Fell Walker

A Danton Cawood book

by

Peter Rankin

Fell Walker by Peter Rankin © 2023

ISBN: 9798871649114

Copyright © 2023 Peter Rankin

All rights reserved

Fell Walker by Peter Rankin © 2023

To Cristina

Without you I would never have
published 'Fell Walker'

Fell Walker by Peter Rankin © 2023

Contents

Chapter One – The Walk 5

Chapter Two – Breakfast 15

Chapter Three – Sleep in 22

Chapter Four – New Friends... 33

Chapter Five – A Chat in the Bar 40

Chapter Six – Going Home.. 49

Chapter Seven – Starting Over 57

Chapter Eight – A grand day out 73

Chapter Nine – A little Chat 84

Chapter ten – The Boss.. 89

Chapter Eleven – Party Time...................................... 94

Chapter Twelve – An Arresting Lunch................... 102

Chapter Thirteen – A New Diary............................. 112

Chapter Fourteen – Visiting Time 119

Chapter Fifteen – Tragedy 127

Chapter Sixteen – Secret Meeting 137

Chapter Seventeen – Just Walking the Dog........... 145

Chapter Eighteen – Labour Day 152

Chapter Nineteen – Easy Rider................................ 156

Fell Walker by Peter Rankin © 2023

Chapter Twenty – A Working Lunch 161

Chapter Twenty One – Bingo 168

Chapter Twenty Two - A little IT Problem 175

Chapter Twenty Three – Cutting Remarks 179

Chapter Twenty Four – A Day of Rest 187

Chapter Twenty Five – Good Cop Bad Cop 192

Chapter Twenty Six – The Bay.............................. 203

Chapter Twenty Seven – Hill Walking 210

Chapter Twenty Eight – Back to School................ 215

Chapter Twenty Nine – Interview.......................... 222

Chapter Thirty – Closure 234

Chapter Thirty One - Promise to keep 242

Chapter Thirty Two – waifs and strays 250

Epilogue 253

Fell Walker by Peter Rankin © 2023

Chapter One – The Walk

Dan Cawood walked along the footpath at the edge of Farndale moor, long ago when the North Yorkshire moors had been pitted with mines the footpath had been a railway line. Today it offered a fantastic view across the top of the moors and down into the lush farm land of the valley below. Ahead of him was just over a miles walk until he reached the pub where he'd booked a room. It was his first bit of luxury for 10 days and 160 miles, he only had two days to go until he finished the coast to coast walk 190 miles across the dales and fells and hills of northern England.

He'd been kept well entertained for the last couple of days, as he had fallen in with a couple from his home town of York. Dan being quiet at the best of times was happy to be regaled with their funny stories and lovey-duvey nature, as he walked happily with this honeymoon couple. They were heading to the Lion Inn on Blakey Ridge, a desolate and beautiful place that had a pub with a great reputation for a warm welcome and good food. The three of them were meeting up with a few more people in the bar tonight, they had all met while walking in the last ten days. An instant camaraderie seemed to spring up between walkers on the coast to coast, after passing by the same faces for a couple days conversations soon sprang up about which

Fell Walker by Peter Rankin © 2023

bit of everyone's body ached the most, where was good for food and how tough yesterday's climb had been.

They were meeting up with Mike a teacher from Rochdale he liked beer and cricket and kept up such a pace that no one else could walk with him. They were also meeting John and Toni two brothers who had lost their mother to cancer last year and these two London boys would have raised over £2,000 for cancer research by the time they hit the east coast. Last but no means least there was Josh a recent recruit to their walking club he was an impoverished American student with a keen sense of humour, he famously told everyone that he would have done the 12 day walk spending just £60, then he sloped off to his tent before it was his round the previous night and everyone could believe it.

Once they reached the pub the young couple ran inside for a drink, but Dan stayed outside stretching his legs. For the last couple of years he hadn't really done as much exercise as he should have. His promotion meant he'd either been tied to a desk or chauffeured around. He had been surprised how unfit he was on the first few days walking, but over the last ten days he felt himself getting fitter and fitter. He also knew he was getting older and spent the next ten minutes stretching out his calves and hamstrings, he'd forgotten to stretch after day one of the walk and it took him half an hour to get his boots on the following morning. Dan took off his rucksack and sat on a bench outside the pub, he reached into his pocket and pulled out a pipe. He put a little tobacco in and struck a match. He leant back sucked on the pipe, kicked out his legs and enjoyed the view. He enjoyed the pipe more than he had ever expected, he was in year eight of his ten year quitting smoking plan, just one pipe every day, and every time he lit his pipe he felt sorry that pretty soon he would have to give it up.

As he sat there smoking his pipe a group of 7 bikers came hurtling towards him across the moor getting louder and louder, then pulled into the car park and skidded to a halt raising a rain of gravel out side the pub. Shit there goes the neighbourhood thought Dan. But, they all got off their bikes holding the base of their spines, most of them had the type of belly that comes from twenty years of good living and when they took their helmets off they had grey hair and trendy glasses. Dan smiled at least he'd had a bike since he was seventeen and the spare tyre round his middle came from beer stress and fast food, these guys were just in the middle of an expensive midlife crisis. They swaggered into the pub with their designer leathers and Harley Davidson saddlebags. They all had BaBY written across their leathers Dan wondered what it stood for Balding and Buying Youth.

Fell Walker by Peter Rankin © 2023

Walking into the pub he was hit by the warmth of the open fires and the smell of steak and kidney pies, Dan's legs were turning to jelly as he walked through the bar. It was a huge cavernous place with a big public bar at the front and a restaurant at the back then beyond that a number of little stairways leading to the bedrooms. The pub had grown almost organically over the past 300 years, it had the kind of charm interior designers try to put into all modern pubs but so very rarely do.

Nostalgia overtook him the place had barely changed in the last 15 years since he had first brought Jenny for her twenty fourth birthday. He wasn't sure if he still missed Jenny or the idea of someone to come home to and moan about his day. They remained friends their life had just drifted apart or rather she had just drifted apart. A few times over the last few days he'd had to really stop himself phoning her up when he saw a fantastic view, and he knew that she would have loved the stoat that stopped ten feet in front of him on the path yesterday it had a look around and scampered off.

Dan had walked across the pub and was stood at the bar in a world of his own, the woman behind the bar repeated her words for the third time, this time very slowly "Excuse me love, can I help you" "yes, yes I'm sorry I was day dreaming " said Dan. "I haven't been here in ages and it just brought back some memories", "when were you last here" asked the barmaid. "fifteen years ago, I brought my ex-wife". "Well Dom and I have had the place for twelve years so I'm afraid that's a bit before my time, some of the regulars won't 'ave been home since then. Now then darlin' what can I get you". She was one of life's natural landladies, short plump and bubbly, but in just a short time Dan could tell she ran the place with a rod of iron. "I've booked a room in the name of Cawood, and I'd like a meal tonight please". "Well the room's fine, but you'll have to get a meal from the bar menu the restaurants full tonight" she said "how would you like to pay" after a few more minutes pleasantries and a laugh at the expense of some of the regulars and another at the expense of Dan, he headed off to his room.

His room was small, but it had fantastic views out over the moors and most importantly of all there was a bath. Normally Dan hated baths he was 6'4" and it normally meant folding himself up and getting his feet and bum wet with a lot of splashing around. This though was a proper bath, a big old deep Victorian cast iron bath. He sat on the bed and pulled his boots off, and went through his daily routine of examining his feet, a habit he'd got into while on exercise in the army. He only had one blister and the Compeed plaster he put on yesterday seemed to be holding up. His boots though were in a bit of a sorry state and if it rained tomorrow the left one was bound to leak. He lay back on the bed and started to doze off, he wanted to eat, sleep and take a bath all at the same time. Dan forced his feet back into their little prisons and headed back downstairs.

He was the last of the group to get down to the bar and despite its size and out of the way location there wasn't a seat in sight. There were families here celebrating birthdays, couples who'd driven out to the country for a romantic weekend, what looked like a small chapter of the hells angels eating fillet steak and camped outside was a school group on a Duke of Edinburgh award expedition. He finally found a seat and with the end of the journey in sight, all the walkers let their hair down.

As the beer flowed jokes were laughed at and stories were told. They found out that when Toni finally built up the courage to come out to his mother she burst his bubble by saying "Oh I've known that for ages, and while were telling secrets I've been having an affair with a married man for the last three years". They found out that Katie couldn't walk after three pints of scrumpy and had to be carried to bed, and also that Mike had a fine singing voice but only knew the words to the neighbours theme tune. Josh complained that everyone in England thought it was his fault that George W Bush was president which really galled him as he hated the man, and of course disappeared to his tent long before he could buy anyone a drink.

Fell Walker by Peter Rankin © 2023

As the night drew on a few of the locals at the bar joined their group and two couples out for a romantic weekend got absorbed as the group spread out over another table in the bar. It was a happy friendly night and everyone was extolling the virtues of northern hospitality despite the fact they were from all over the country. Jack a local farmer had a look at their maps and pointed out a detour that would give them a fantastic view in the morning. They learnt from the landlady that Jack propped up the bar every night and he never fed his dog as it lived on scraps, crisps and beer that it got off the tourists.

The night was moving along wonderfully there was a great atmosphere in the bar everyone was well fed and watered. There was a real sense of having accomplished something among the little group of walkers, and a devil may care attitude to the fact they would be walking with throbbing heads in the morning. The drink had washed away the pain in Dan's feet and back, and good company had kept him from his bed.

At 11:30 Dan decided enough was enough and that he must have a bath before going to bed he owed it to his feet and his back. At that point the door swung open with a mighty bang everyone stopped what they were doing and stared as a short redhead in her early fifties struggled with an enormous holdall into the bar, she looked around the bar and she spotted a balding man of roughly the same age as Dan with a weather beaten outdoors face in the corner, she strode over to the table and said "I'm not putting up with you and your crap anymore" she stabbed at him with her finger "I don't care what people think anymore, take your clothes and just piss off" and she threw the bag at him, he stood quickly and grabbed her forearms pushing her backward till the wall brought her to a halt "Calm down" he said almost a whisper. "Calm Fuckin' Down Calm Fuckin' Down, I'm not putting up with this shit again" there was a real anger in her eyes, as she spat the words at him.

By this time the landlady was on her feet and ringing the bell she kept behind the bar to call last orders, when the ringing stopped the whole bar was silent and didn't know whether to stare at the stunned couple or the landlady in full flight, she marched down the bar, stopped and very slowly, calmly and quietly looked at them both and said "This is a family pub and you're not welcome here I'd like you to leave please", if her daughter was there she would have told everyone in the bar if she shouts you're OK, but when she does the calm, quiet voice just run. The short redhead pushed the man back and to his surprise he ended up sat on his backside on the floor "I've said all I came to say, you can keep this piece of crap" she said as she kicked out at the man on the floor and ran out of the bar in tears.

Fell Walker by Peter Rankin © 2023

The man stared at the landlady dumbstruck, everyone in the bar was gob smacked, the whole thing had happened in seconds'. As they sat there in silence they could hear gravel being dug up in the car park and then the roar of an engine but within seconds it was out of earshot. Again the landlady looked at the man on the floor and slowly and calmly said "I'd like you to leave, please". "But… but I can't" stammered the man "You don't have any choice there is nowhere for you here, get out" the landlady remained calm but there was now a trace of anger in her voice as she pointed at the door, "I can't" replied the man "I've got a group of school children camping outside". The landlady stared at him for a long time and then stared at the wall where he had just been standing and finally said "OK you can stay but I don't want anymore trouble" the man got up slowly and walked over to his table, picked up his keys and turned round with the eyes of the pub on him and said "I'm really sorry about this, I don't know what happened just then. Honestly" He turned with his tail between his legs, picked up the holdall and walked off towards the bedrooms.

Just as the man turned the corner out of sight of the bar, someone picked up their pint and said "Woodpecker what a refreshing change" everyone in the room burst out laughing a quick flurry of jokes and laughs ensued. Mostly about divorce, and being under the thumb. Dan stayed for awhile longer to laugh at others misery and his own divorce, but the bar had closed and he really wanted a bath so headed on upstairs.

Once in his room he was gutted it was midnight and there was no hot water, so he sat on the end of his bed and forced himself to drink two pints of water, otherwise he would have the biggest hangover in the morning. He set his alarm for 6:30am, the next day he was going to have his bath before breakfast and still manage an early start. He went into the bathroom and washed his face, he stared at himself in the mirror. Ever since he'd gone bald three years ago he'd started to shave his whole head including the moustache he'd had since he was 21. He had been pretty feral for the last 10 days and was now sporting a full but messy beard and had some short dark hair around the sides of his head. While the top was of his head was a reddish brown sunburnt colour from being outside for the last 10 days, he regretted instantly not wearing a hat on the walk if he shaved his head now he would look like a barbers pole. He lay on the bed and thought about taking off his clothes.

Chapter Two – Breakfast

BEEP BEEP BEEP BEEP his hand shot out from under the duvet and repeatedly hit the top of the alarm clock until it stopped. Dan was disorientated he hated waking up in strange places, even though he did it so often. He'd been beaten up by the urban gorilla again it had kicked him in the stomach, punched him in the head, stolen all his money and then just before it left it crapped in his mouth. In his twenties two pints of water just before bed guaranteed no hang over, now heading towards forty it just meant waking up alive. Dan went into the bathroom, it took an age to fill the bath and the sound of rushing water hurt the inside of his eyes. He turned out his rucksack on the bed, found his first aid kit and gulped down two Nurofen. Eventually he slipped into the bath, he stayed there almost motionless for nearly an hour letting hot water trickle into the bath while cold water ran out of the overflow pipe.

By the time breakfast was served at 8:30 he was down stairs dressed and hungry. The little group of walkers sat together minus Josh who couldn't afford Bed and Breakfast and so camped outside. They took bets on whether Mr under the thumb would come down for breakfast, every table was talking about the events of last night. The restaurant was full of people who looked like Dan felt.

Fell Walker by Peter Rankin © 2023

It was a super breakfast just what Dan wanted to mop up the beer a full English, with black pudding, fried bread and washed down with a pint of tea "Well To-To you know your in Yorkshire now" he said to himself as he took his first bite of sausage.

All through breakfast there had been no sign of 'Mr Under the Thumb' and Dan snacked on toast that he ate because it was there. He invited the little group of walkers to his cottage in Robin Hood's Bay, their destination at the end of the walk, he would sort out the Barbeque (the local butcher did great sausages) if they brought the beer. Everyone took out mobile phones and numbers and E-mail addresses were swapped. Tonight they were all staying in different villages so there would be no repeat of last nights boozy-do, which was good as Dan didn't think he could cope with a another night on the piss.

There was still a lot of food on the buffet so Dan got another plate of egg and bacon and made it up into sandwiches. Wrapped them in a napkin on his knee under the table, and when none of the staff were looking he put them in the pocket of his fleece on the back of his chair. He took the sandwiches outside and into the sheep field that doubled as a campsite. There in the corner was Josh's little green tent, it was old and dirty and wouldn't have looked out of place on the news to show the conditions in some third world refugee camp. Dan only wished he had the time to do some real travelling but, if he had the time to go travelling he definitely didn't have the money. He wandered over and wondered what the etiquette for knocking on the door of a tent was. "Huh-Hum are you in there" Dan said, after a few seconds a happy but tired face looked out at him "How goes it man?" said Josh, as the laid back Californian got out of the tent in just his boxers and his straggly hair and beard and stretched to his full height, about the same as Dan but definitely thinner. "Great, I thought you could do with a bit of brekkie so I took what was left of the buffet" Dan said as he handed over the pile of sandwiches "That's excellent, thanks man, I spent yesterdays food money on a packet of tobacco" he said as he launched into the pile of food. With a mouthful of food he offered Dan a cup of tea so long as he liked it black without sugar, but Dan was prepared he had grabbed a pocket full of milk cartons from the buffet table in the restaurant just in case he wanted to make a cuppa at lunchtime. "Man, a hot meal and milk in my tea, all I need is a bath and this is gonna' be a perfect day", "Okay if there's no staff around, come up to my room and use the bath" said Dan "Man, I'm starting to worry about you" Josh said as he smiled the sort of cheeky smile only the young and beautiful can get away with.

Dan and Josh spent the next half hour drinking tea, Josh smoked his roll ups and Dan sat there sniffing the air longing for a cigarette, at least he thought I eventually got a drink out of Josh. It turned out that it hadn't just been an eventful night in the pub but out here in the field as well. "Man last night was fucked up, the guy in that blue tent snored like a pig, those high school kids they were in and out of each others tents till 4:30am, then someone started kicking ass in those sheds over there and then a bloody sheep woke me at 6am". It turned out Josh had just finished his PhD in chemical engineering at Nottingham University and wanted to do some environmental research work. His father worked in London at the US embassy and he was trying see as much of Europe as he could before he had to go home in a couple of month's time. Josh said he liked going to new places but the best part of travel was meeting new people and just the buzz of the experience. "Say hi to old glory from me when you get home" requested Dan, "You been over the pond, big man" said Josh, "loads of times, in fact I've got dual nationality my father was a Yank and I see my granddad when ever I can", "hell, I knew you weren't no real limey when you gave me breakfast" said Josh with a grin and the best redneck accent the could muster. Dan invited Josh to his cottage in Robin Hood's Bay when the walk was over for the barbeque, he liked this poor but amiable rogue and Josh ended up inviting himself to stay at the cottage in the Bay for a couple of nights.

Fell Walker by Peter Rankin © 2023

Dan was quite happy he wouldn't have to spend two nights alone in his little hide away. It would be the first time he'd been to the Bay since his divorce, the little cottage was the first house he and Jenny had bought together it was supposed to be an investment for when he was posted abroad. But, they had fallen in love with the place and never actually got round to renting it out, just spending a fortune coming up from London for the weekend whenever they could. His mum used the place more than he did now, he really liked the Bay he always felt calm and centred whenever he went there. As a child it had been his mum's and his place, then it became His and Jenny's place, now he still hoped it would still be his place. He had spent the last twelve months feeling lost, this walk was something he had wanted to do for years he hoped that ending up in the Bay would make him feel centred again.

Dan wandered out into the fields to look down at the valley below, he felt a bit melancholy. Josh had everything ahead of him, while Dan felt the best he had was behind him, a divorced wife he didn't know if he still loved anymore, a career and a lifestyle that he loved, all gone. Jenny Dan's ex-wife had become resentful of his job in the army about four years ago, just her own career was taking off. After years of arguing Dan finally caved in and resigned his commission, it was either the job or his marriage, only to discover Jenny hadn't just moved past the army but had moved past Dan as well. So here he was nearly forty starting all over again even living back at his mum's.

Dan left the field and headed back to his room to pack his rucksack, he felt a bit unsteady on his feet but at least his headache had been washed away. In his room he couldn't believe it, his map was nowhere to be seen he realised that last night everyone was using it to look at tomorrows walk. So he went down into the bar and got down on his hands and knees to look around where they were sat last night.

Josh came into the bar checking their were no staff around and was a little bemused to see Dan sprawled out on the floor reaching under furniture and swearing as all he could find were antique fluff balls. "Hey man, any chance of that bath" whispered Josh, Dan looked up from his search Josh was carrying the dirtiest towel he had ever seen and a tiny scrap of soap. "Here's my key it's room 7 upstairs, and for god sake use one of the pub towels you'll get impetigo if you use that bloody thing" Dan said pointing at the towel, "I've lost my bloody map, can you believe it". "Have you asked at the bar?" Questioned Josh "No I haven't actually would you mind asking for me" replied Dan "Sure thing and if they haven't I'll see if they can Xerox mine, cos' at your age you really shouldn't be on your knees" he said with a grin and wandered off to find a member of staff.

Fell Walker by Peter Rankin © 2023

Chapter Three – Sleep in

Just as Dan had given up the search for the map a teenage girl came into the pub and very nervously started looking around. He recognised her as one of the 'high school kids' that Josh had been talking about earlier. Dan walked over and said "hi there, the toilets are just through that archway on the left", "thanks, but I'm looking for someone" she replied. Dan was just about to go and pack it was just after 10:30am and he had wanted to be on the road at 9am, when his inquisitive nature got the better of him "Can I help, who are looking for?" he enquired, "Mr Carter, our teacher he said he would be out before 10 this morning, to see if we were OK ", he realised she had her rucksack, boots and waterproofs on, there was probably a group of kids ready for the off outside. "What does Mr Carter look like" said Dan, "Oh Carty, he's really old and bald and a bit fat" and blushed having realised what she'd said. "Has he got a sun tanned weather beaten face?" enquired Dan "yeah suppose so" was the reply. "I think I know who you mean, he was staying in the pub last night but he didn't come down for breakfast, come on lets see if we can find him" and Dan headed after Josh to find one of the staff, eventually they had to ring the bell for attention as there was no-one to be seen.

Fell Walker by Peter Rankin © 2023

It took about five minutes for someone to turn up, and the school girl was obviously apprehensive about talking to strange men while they waited at the bar. Eventually the landlady appeared, it seemed that mornings weren't her thing or she hadn't put her make up on yet. "Yes darling what do you want?" she said, "This young lady is missing her teacher and I've a feeling he was the gentleman you spoke to late last night in the bar, I just wondered if you knew where he was", "No I haven't seen him" she said as she flicked through the booking diary "and he hasn't checked out or paid yet, he better not have done a bloody runner". Dan didn't think he would have done, he knew from his own recent past that when it's going tits up at home you try and put a brave face on at work and not let anyone know. "What room is he in?" asked Dan, "Room 8" replied the landlady. "That's next to mine I'll pop up and see if he's slept in" said Dan to the girl.

Dan and Josh went upstairs there were only three rooms on his little corridor. Josh went for his much needed bath and Dan banged on the door to room 8, there was no reply.

The locks to all the rooms were pretty rudimentary old Yale locks, Dan went back into his room emptied out his first aid kit again and took the thin sheet of aluminium that was an emergency signal mirror, no wonder he was skint he'd paid £20 for this three years ago and never used it, he just couldn't resist gear. Dan went back to the door to room 8, slipped the thin sheet of aluminium between the door and the frame pushed a little and heard the lock click open. "Too easy" Dan said to himself, he turned the handle and let the door open.

There on the bed under the duvet was the unmoving school teacher. Dan walked into the room carefully, he'd seen enough dead men to know he was about to inspect a corpse. But, in hope he felt the neck for a pulse anyway which he didn't find. He looked at the man's face, blue lips, he reached down and pulled open one of the man's eyes with his thumb, burst blood vessels. "Oh Shit!" Dan said to himself, he turned and looked where he had walked into the room and tried to use the same footprints to extract himself from the scene.

Dan went back into his room and took his phone out of his bag, no signal. He banged on the door to the bathroom "Yeah" shouted Josh, "Listen, get out of the bath go to the bottom of the stairs and don't let anyone come up" said Dan and ran downstairs without waiting for a reply.

Dan rushed into the bar one of the East European waitresses from breakfast was polishing glasses. Dan said "The man in room 8 is dead, I need to use the phone". The waitress dropped the glass, put the phone on the bar and then ran off.

By the time the landlord and the landlady came running into the bar Dan had phoned 999. The landlady shouted "What the hell's goin' on", Dan just put up his hand signalling for silence and said into the phone "This is Detective Sergeant Cawood of the North Yorkshire Police, and yes I am sure the man has been suffocated" there a minutes silence while Dan listened to whoever was on the other end of the phone. "Is there no-one closer, are you sure you can't get anyone out here faster than that, time is critical here it is almost certainly foul play".

Dan put the phone down and looked at the landlady "The gentleman in room 8 is dead, I've been into his room and I suspect some foul play" as usual when he was concentrating on what he was saying his hands were trying to describe what he was saying, as though he was holding an imaginary football in front of him. The landlord tried to interrupt, but after years of command Dan just spoke as though the man didn't exist, this was Dan's world and he knew what he was doing. "The police and emergency services are on there way here now, but it's going to be some time before they arrive, no one must leave and no-one must go up the stairs to room 8". The landlord was red in the face at having been interrupted, "look we've got a bloody pub to run, lets just wait for the rossas to get 'ere" he blurted out at Dan. Calm and in control Dan looked at him and said "The rossas are here I'm Detective Sergeant Cawood of the North Yorkshire Police, we need to leave the body until a forensic team can get here, no-one can leave because the police will want to interview everyone, and you can consider the building under the control of the police for at least the rest of the day" with every point Dan made he stabbed the air with his forefinger. Again the landlord tried to interrupt Dan, but he put the same finger up to stop the landlord in his tracks. Dan may have been a bit out of shape but he was still an imposing figure, he drew himself to his full height and stared at the landlord, then very quietly and calmly but still stabbing the air with his finger he said "That man is someone's son, more than likely he's someone's husband and someone's father and today they haven't just lost a days takings, I think you need to reflect on that" the landlord stayed silent for a few seconds and then said "yeah I'm sorry this just hasn't happened to us before". "I realise it's a lot to take in but we must be practical" said Dan.

Within minutes Dan was organising everyone, all the campers had come in from outside and the guests had come down from their rooms. The landlord Dom went into his office and got a box of pens a packet of paper and the security video tape from inside the bar. The landlady Elaine phoned people to tell them there had been a burst pipe and the flood damage meant they would not be open for the rest of the week, she hoped they would understand and it wouldn't put them off coming to the pub in future. One of the Eastern European girls who acted as cleaner, chamber maid and waitress made coffee lots of coffee.

Dan sat everyone down in the restaurant as spread out as far as possible and said to them all "There was an incident upstairs last night and as some of you will have heard, a man has died. The police are on their way but won't be here for some time, in order to make it as easy as possible for them when they arrive I suggest you all write down your actions and memories from last night and this morning, please don't talk to anyone about last night until you've done this" Dan knew from bitter experience that a good and reliable witness was open to suggestion just to be more helpful. "Write down your name, date of birth, address and phone number on the paper, hopefully if you do this it will mean that when the police do get here you will be delayed you for the shortest possible time". Dan knew that with so many people in the building and some of them under 18 no-one was leaving early today, but at least the writing task would focus their minds and give them something to do.

Fell Walker by Peter Rankin © 2023

While everyone was waiting for the police Dan grabbed a couple of disposable cameras from behind the bar, some freezer bags from the kitchen and headed back to his room. He knew that the SOCO (scene of crime officer) wouldn't be happy that he went into the room, but evidence had a sell by date, body fats evaporated, smells drifted away, bodies decomposed and chemicals breakdown into their component parts.

Dan needed to be as sterile as possible if he was going back into the room 8, he also didn't want anyone to know he was going back in so he would have to break in again. He went into his room and emptied out his rucksack and first aid kit, then grabbed a couple of plastic disposable shower caps form the bathroom the kind that no-one ever uses but they put in all hotel rooms anyway. Sealed in a plastic bag at the bottom of his rucksack was his emergency dry gear there was a brand new pair of long johns and thermal vest in there that he'd bought especially for this trip. Dan stripped naked dressed in the thermal underwear, put the shower caps on his feet, and donned a pair of latex gloves from his first aid kit. He knew he looked an absolute plonker, but there was no-one here to see him. In the plastic bag that held his dry gear he put some paper, a couple of pens, the disposable cameras, freezer bags, his torch and the tweezers, tape and thermometer from his first aid kit.

Dan picked up the bag and signal mirror and proceeded to break into room 8 again. Once he had the door open he took out one of the disposable cameras and took a couple of shots. He put the camera back and as carefully as he could Dan went into the room stopping after step to look around.

Just like his room, it was simple enough there was an old chest of drawers, a wardrobe and a bed with shelf above that acted as a bedside table and light stand, everything was clean but dusty. Mr Carter obviously wasn't using the drawers or the wardrobe, he had a small but neatly packed rucksack at the foot of his bed. Dan could tell he was a fastidious man he hadn't needed to empty his rucksack out to get at what he wanted, and as he got nearer the bed he could see crisply ironed pyjamas under the duvet, in fact the bed was almost made, when Dan woke in morning he'd often found the duvet on the floor and even occasionally out of it's cover, something Jenny always complained about.

Once next to the bed Dan took more photos, With blue lips and white sheets and pillows Mr Carter looked peaceful as though he had fallen asleep in a bank of snow. Luckily the cameras had a flash and Dan had to wait between shots so they could recharge, which gave him time to look around. Then very carefully he lifted the duvet and folded it at the man's waist so that he could see his pyjama top. He spent some time looking at the corpse tracking the entire length of the body examining it inch by inch. On the breast pocket of his pyjama top there were two very long auburn hairs. Dan took a photo then picked up the hairs with his tweezers put them into a freezer bag and wrote a quick note describing the position of the hairs and the time they were found. He held the bag up to the light, there on the end of one hair was a follicular tag, a tiny piece of flesh that contained enough DNA to tell Dan exactly who it belonged to "Got ya" he said.

Dan took out the thermometer from his bag he carefully checked the corpse and then lifted the collar of the pyjamas he slid his hand under the cotton trying not to disturb the man's chest and slipped the thermometer into Mr Carter's armpit.

Dan went into the bathroom, it really was Mr Carter's unlucky night he only had a shower. The bathroom was tidy with a few toiletries on the back of the sink, there was some white powder on the floor and Dan suspected it was talc but took out the tape from his bag and tore off a couple of strips, he patted the powder with the sticky side of the tape then put it in one of the freezer bags with another quickly scribbled note. There were some clothes hanging on a coat hanger on the back of the door, Dan frisked them quickly with a practised hand there were some keys but no money, papers, or a wallet.

Dan went back into the bedroom there was no sign of a wallet in the top of the rucksack or any of side pockets, by the look of it just a few good outer clothes, a map, provisions and a first aid kit. It was the rucksack of someone who was confident and experienced outdoors. Up against the wall by the door was the large holdall that had been brought into the pub last night, Dan unzipped it, it seemed to be full of rags, he took out one from the top and realised it was a good dress shirt that had been attacked with a pair of scissors. The bag was full of what once had been very expensive clothes 'a woman scorned' thought Dan.

He went back over to the body carefully lifted the corner of the pyjamas and extracted the thermometer it read 94 degrees Fahrenheit, he quickly put it on the shelf that doubled as a bed side table next to an alarm clock and took a photo. Dan found it was easier to estimate time of death working in Fahrenheit, most people run at 98.6F and when they die lose one to one and a half degrees every hour depending on ambient conditions. The clock read nearly eleven thirty and Mr Carter must have died between four and a half and seven hours ago. That put time of death between four thirty and seven this morning.

Fell Walker by Peter Rankin © 2023

Dan packed everything away into the plastic bag that he'd brought into the room and the hairs and powder too. He had one last look around the room and got down on his hands and knees to check under the bed. There stuffed under the door side of the bed was a yellow pillow, it had the impression of a foot on it as though it had been kicked under the bed. Dan took out the camera again and finished off the roll of film. He crawled closer to the bed and examined the yellow pillow further, there was a distinct foot tread on the pillow and another auburn hair trapped between the pillow and bed. Dan bagged the second hair no follicular tag this time, then he headed back to his room to get changed he just hoped there was no-one on the corridor to see him.

Chapter Four – New Friends

Once back in his shorts and tee shirt Dan carefully put his bag of evidence at the bottom of his wardrobe and headed back downstairs. In the bar most people had finished writing and were sitting around drinking coffee and chatting. Dan took everyone's statements and photocopied them in the pub office. He organised them into groups; the coast to coasters he glanced at but he'd been with them all night and morning; the staff had cleared up last night had a drink and gone to bed; most other guests ate, drank and slept in that order and the school children had been in bed for 10pm and slept the whole night through. Dan went back upstairs and put the original statements with the evidence.

On his return to the bar Dan found the local bobbies had arrived a sergeant and police constable were stood in the bar, he went over and introduced himself to the sergeant who asked for some ID and Dan thought how trusting you're the first to ask for it "This say's your DI Cawood of the Met" the sergeant said sternly, "that's right I'm transferring to North Yorkshire to be nearer my mum, in fact I'm not due to start here till next Monday, I'm on holiday".

When Jenny had given Dan an ultimatum "the army or me", Dan chose Jenny she was the only woman he had ever loved, and even with the divorce going through he was still a little besotted with her. Dan resigned his commission and looked around for another job. During his time with 'The Branch' in London he had a lot of contact with the Met and was owed a few favours, he had arranged to join the Metropolitan Police through the backdoor.

After a short course at Hendon where they didn't teach Dan anything but reminded him how much he hated training courses. He had two months on the beat as a probationer, mainly sat in steamed up police cars or manning check points looking for Al Qaeda. Then he was made up to detective sergeant, Dan had hardly warmed the seat in his office when Jenny said "Dan I love you, but we just don't work any more" she wanted to be friends but not lovers. They had both cried a lot that night, it was the last time he'd spent the night in the same bed as someone, ever since then he'd felt lonely and lost. Staying in the same house as Jenny, he found really painful so Dan put in for a transfer to York and home.

"Well you've really brought the bloody sun with you haven't ya" said the sergeant, he was a big bluff Yorkshire man a little taller even than Dan although not as broad, he was also a little older than Dan and had a full head of white hair and a white beard. "Right then let's start on the paper work otherwise we'll be here forever, who found the body" continued the sergeant. "I did, he missed a meeting with the school group he was in charge of so I broke into his room. It's the one next to mine" said Dan. The sergeant shook his head and said "bloody hell, you don't do things by halves do ya. You're right int thick of this aren't ya".

Dan and the sergeant went upstairs and looked through the door at the corpse, Dan explained to the sergeant who was here last night and what measures he had put in place to stop people from leaving, he thought better of telling him about going into the room he already thought he was top of his list of suspects.

Sergeant George James turned out to be a jovial character, he and Dan went down stairs to wait. George explained that normally there would be a DI in Malton but due to staffing shortages there wasn't one available so they would have to wait for one to come over from HQ in York. They drank coffee and flicked through the statements everyone had written, they'd done all they could, now they had to wait.

At twelve thirty the police doctor arrived he put on his sterile paper overalls latex gloves and shoe covers then went upstairs to declare John Carter dead, he had only been in the pub 2 minutes when outside 3 cars arrived in convoy.

There were two Ford Focuses and a Citroen van. The first car was a focus it contained two men both in their early thirties wearing cheap suits and the shorter of the two was sporting a moustache. If you looked up plain clothes policemen in the dictionary there would have been a picture of these two, the short one jumped out of the car and lit up a cigarette. In the second car was a man and a woman, the man wore a suit it wasn't cheap like the others it was a very nice grey wool suit, but no shirt and tie underneath just a plain black turtle neck. The way he held himself when he got out of the car Dan knew he was in charge. With him was a very pretty girl she wore an elegant trouser suit and definitely didn't look like a copper. The closer she got to Dan who by now was in the car park outside the pub the prettier she got, she had a beautiful dark complexion almost Indian. Lastly out of the van stepped a man in police uniform carrying a solid looking case, he looked a few years older than Dan, and from his shape Dan could tell he hadn't walked the beat in along time.

Dan and Sergeant George James waited by the door to the pub in the car park while the five policemen walked towards them. The tall well dressed man was the first to reach them and confidently said "Hello I'm DI King and this is DC Wheeler, DC Jones acting DS Bush and PC Garner" as he waved his left hand in the others general direction. Dan could tell that he didn't think it important they knew anyone else's name but his, he was here now and he was in charge. Dan couldn't make out the man's accent but it was somewhere down south but not London.

"I'm Sergeant James this is Dan an off duty copper who found the corpse, the doctor is upstairs with the body now" said George. "Right Bushy you see what these two know, Johno Jonesy you have a word with all the yokels in there" said DI King as he pointed through the window into the bar "and Jimmy you and me are gonna get suited up and see the body". Immediately Dan disliked this man he put a -y on the end of everyone's name as if they were in the England cricket team. He had been in the army long enough to know he was a bully.

It seemed that 'Bushy' was acting detective sergeant Bush and was the prettiest policeman Dan had ever seen in his life. Trying not to be obvious Dan looked her up and down she was very pretty and had an athletic figure Dan guessed she was about 5'2". As he looked he saw a wedding ring "Ah! Shit" he said under his breath, "what was that" asked DS Bush. She and George had been discussing what he knew about the events of last night. "Oh a ah, nothing!" said Dan he felt himself going bright red.

Dan left DS Bush and Sergeant James to it and went in the pub. He thought he'd better find DI King and tell him what he had done while he was waiting. The two detectives in the bar were trying to get everyone's

Fell Walker by Peter Rankin © 2023

name it looked like pandemonium with everyone trying to give information in the hope that they would be allowed to leave. The only person who looked happy was Josh, he was drinking hot coffee and eating sandwiches, if Josh was travelling for the buzz of experience he was certainly getting it today. Dan slipped through the bar unnoticed and on to the stairs leading up to room eight.

Dan walked quietly along the corridor and could hear a conversation "So when do you get your new DS" said the doctor, by now Dan was outside room 8 and the door was open. Inside was the doctor, DI King and the out of shape policeman. They were all dressed alike in sterile over suits, plastic shoe covers and latex gloves, a 'scene suit'. The Doctor had a bag and the out of shape policeman had a camera, Dan thought he must be the SOCO (scene of crimes officer). All three of them were all on their knees around the bed with their backs to Dan. "Bloody Hell I don't even want my new DS he's some French army wanker who can't hack it in the Met" said the DI. Dan coughed so they would know he was there, they all turned quickly. DI King was quickly on his feet and striding towards Dan as he said "Oi fuckwit, who the hell do you think you are marching into my crime scene". The DI was standing in front of Dan trying to be menacing, but he stood a good six inches shorter than Dan and while he was in good shape he looked a bit puny stood next to Dan.

'He's not even a six footer' Dan thought and smiled then said "Some French army wanker who can't hack it in the Met sir. I'm DS Danton Cawood and I should be reporting for duty next Monday in York, however given what's happened in the last twenty four hours I can take it my leave will be cut short". DI King shook his head and said "please tell me this is a fucking joke".

Dan waited outside the room for the next 30 minutes until its three occupants had finished processing the scene, when DI King and the SOCO came out of the room Dan took them into his room explained what he had done earlier in the morning and gave them the plastic bag from the bottom of his wardrobe. DI King was angry that Dan had interfered, but Dan could tell he was also impressed at his swift action. The SOCO PC Dave "but people call me Jimmy" Garner, carefully looked through everything in the bag and said "this is irregular but useable gov".

Dan sorted out the statements by groups of people and handed them to DI King explaining who was who and giving a quick run down of their contents. Then he told his new DI about the events of last night and the redhead in the bar.

Fell Walker by Peter Rankin © 2023

Chapter Five – A Chat in the Bar

DI King took Dan down stairs and introduced him to the rest of the team. DC John Wheeler was the shorter of the other two detectives he spoke with an Essex estuary grunge accent, moaned constantly that his mobile phone didn't have signal and sucked the life out his cigarettes. DC David Jones despite his name spoke with a broad West Riding accent he often pronounced d's as t's and so Dan reckoned he must be from around Bradford, he seemed a quiet man who was happy to remain in the background. Acting DS Bush would lose her temporary promotion now that Dan had turned up, despite that she seemed pleased to meet him, she was Nazy Bush, it was an Iranian name but she had the kind of nondescript accent you only get from 15 years in the army or five years at boarding school. 'Jimmy' Garner remained upstairs to sort some loose ends.

DC Jones was sent out to the car to get some tape recorders, pads of paper and pens. Then DI King sat them all down and said now Dan was here he was to start working for a living. They were to interview everyone who had spent last night at the pub and the DI decided to divide and conquer, and handed out Dan's notes. He would take the bikers, DC Bush the school pupils, DC's Jones and Wheeler would interview the rest of the guests and Dan got the pub staff. Then the DI asked Sergeant James and the PC to search the area around the pub, he asked like they would be doing him a favour but the tone of his voice said it was a command.

They wandered back into the bar and DI King announced that he was sorry but everyone would have to give a statement to one of his staff and then if everything was in order they could all leave.

The DI wandered over to where the bikers were playing cards and said "right you lot, lets get you shifted over there" and pointed to the empty tables at the back of the pub "and I think we'll have some ID while were at it". One of the bikers stood up and gave the DI a real dressing down, he asked about civil rights and quoted proper police procedure and the human rights act. It turned out that BaBY stood for Barrister Bikers of Yorkshire. All the policemen in the pub had a grin from ear to ear, except for DI King whose face was redder than a baboon's bottom.

Dan took the staff into the Licences flat and sat them all down in the living room, it turned out that the only staff on site last night were Dom and Elaine who spent the night together in their flat with their Five year old daughter Bella, and the two Polish waitresses who lived in one of the guest rooms.

Dan interviewed the Polish girls first, they were both from Gdansk and had come to England together as soon as Poland joined the EU 2004, to find work and save money. They arrived in Leeds and worked as cleaners for an agency, they saw this job advertised in the Yorkshire Post and had been living in the pub for nearly 10 months. They said the Landlord and landlady had been really good to them, giving them a free room and helping them to learn English. Dan wasn't surprised they were two pretty girls who worked their socks off and to top it all they had a good rapport with the customers. In fact Anka had a boyfriend in Rosedale, he was one of the locals in the pub last night and Dan didn't think it would be long before her and Janna were Yorkshire housewives. Both Anka and Janna had been working last night in the restaurant and had come into the bar for a drink when they had finished their shift. They had both gone to bed before the mad lady came into the pub last night but Dom told them all about it this morning. They were both up at 6:30 preparing veg for lunch and then they were the waitresses at breakfast. Neither of them could remember seeing the victim yesterday and didn't hear anything through the night.

Dan wished he could talk to these pretty young girls for longer, they had a real naive charm and within minutes he found himself wrapped up in their world. But, in Dan's line of work you have to find out who the scumbags are and then spend some time with them if you want to get anywhere.

Elaine was a Leeds lass born and bred, she had met Dom at a school disco when she was fifteen. After school he had trained as mechanic and she as a Dental Nurse, they got married 1992 when she was twenty. They both wanted to run a pub and so did some relief work for a couple of the major breweries and came out to run the Lion twelve years ago for two months between tenants. That had fallen through and they'd been here ever since. They'd been trying for a baby for ten years and Bella was a product of IVF five years ago.

Last night all the other staff had left and so they cleaned the bar then sat down in their flat and had a glass of brandy before going to bed at around one. Dom was up at 6:30 this morning to start breakfast, and Elaine stayed in bed, Bella came into their room at 7:30 and the two of them watched Disney films in bed until 10, and just after that Elaine came down to the bar and saw Dan.

After his interviews Dan went back into the bar there were still a lot of people who hadn't made a statement so Dan offered to help out. The school children were under sixteen and with the death of Mr Carter didn't have a responsible adult with them so they couldn't be interviewed; DS Bush had spent the last 40 minutes baby sitting them. By now all the children knew Mr

Carter was dead some of them were stunned and the rest were crying.

Dan took over baby sitting duties and DS Bush smoothed some barristers' feathers. He grabbed a cup of tea and sat next to the girl who had come looking for Mr. Carter earlier. There were four boys and four girls sat around one of the tables in the bar they were all stunned and a couple of them were crying apart from the girl Dan sat next to.

Dan said "are you OK?" "suppose so" replied the girl. "My Name's Dan Cawood, is there anything I can get for any of you" "Nah were alright" said the girl, "what's your name" enquired Dan "Suzie".

Dan eventually got chatting to Suzie and found out they were a School group from the lakes and were on their Duke of Edinburgh award silver expedition. They were to spend three days and two nights walking from Osmotherly to Whitby. "Why don't you do your walking in the Lakes" asked Dan, "Health and safety" replied Suzie. It turned out that because the hills were at a higher altitude in the Lakes then someone in a suit had decided they must be really dangerous, so although these children probably walked to school every morning they weren't allowed to walk on the same paths if they had spent days preparing themselves.

Fell Walker by Peter Rankin © 2023

Dan hated health and safety, during his last few years in the army civilian consultants had come in at great expense and told them how to comply with health and safety legislation, they got wrist rests for computers, ergonomically designed mugs and lots of paper work. Which was great when you're in dear old blighty, but not quite so good when you're hiding in an Afghan sewer with 20 people intent on killing you, it's then you wish they'd spent the money on some desent body armour.

"I'm gonna stretch my legs outside, does anyone fancy a breath of fresh air" Dan said to the children. Only Suzie took him up on the offer the rest of the school group sat in a stunned silence. When Dan got outside he stretched out his back and then lit his pipe. "That's hardly a breath of fresh air, is it?" said Suzie. She'd been the one sent into the pub earlier to find Mr Carter and the only one in her little group who had talked to anyone, she may have been only 5'2" but she was obviously brave.

Dan and Suzie started chatting and eventually Dan enquired "Did you know Mr Carter well?" "He's never taught me, but I've done D of E with him since Easter" "So what was Mr Carter like?" asked Dan "He was OK, but he always had favourites" said Suzie. "So you weren't teacher's pet then" said Dan, "Nah, Justin the little lad with the black hair who's crying, he could get off anything, never got done for nothing" replied Suzie. Suzie eyes lit up and conspiratorially she moved closer to Dan and whispered "He nearly got sacked last year, for hitting a pupil" "who was that then?" Dan replied in a hushed voice. "David Wilkes, he did it with his step daughter, and he found out and slapped him in the face in the main corridor at school" Suzie said with real excitement. "How old's his daughter?" asked Dan "Debbie's in year 11 now, so she'd have been 14 or 15 then". "Does his daughter go to your school" asked Dan "Yeah, the whole family's there, Mrs Carter works in the kitchen, she's really weird" Said Suzie, she obviously liked a good gossip but then again so did Dan it was how he did his job. "What's weird about Mrs Carter then?" Asked Dan, "Dinner Ginner, she's the catering manager, she's been really into this Jamie Oliver stuff. She's always puttin' posters up and comin' into PSHE, she's you know really creepy" whispered Suzie.

So Mrs Carter's got red hair thought Dan "Do you hang round with Debbie" Dan probed for a little more information, "No way she's a Goth" said Suzie then laughed to herself "She's a fat Goth, it's really funny her two mates are rexics and everyone calls them the one-o-one gang". Dan smiled he knew when you were 14 there was no greater crime than being different.

Fell Walker by Peter Rankin © 2023

Just then a phone started to ring in Suzie's pocket, she answered it, it was her mother. Suzie spent the next 5 minutes calming her mother down explaining that everything was OK and the headmaster was coming to collect them in the school minibus. When Suzie put the phone down Dan asked how she had signal, "it's not my phone two of the boys are on orange and they've got signal so they let everyone use them" said Suzie. Dan tapped out his pipe on the sole of his boots and then he and Suzie headed back inside.

During the afternoon interviews were conducted and statements carefully filed away. The local undertaker came and took the body to York. The headmaster of the school group arrived in the school minibus with a number of concerned parents, it was decided that they had been through enough today and an officer would go to Keswick in the next few days and take a statement if it was necessary.

Eventually all the guests had left the pub and the staff were tidying up the bar, Jimmy Garner had sealed off the corridor to room 8 and Sergeant George James had come in from outside having found nothing. It was starting to get dark outside and the group of policemen sat and had their first rest in eight hours, anyone who wasn't driving had a pint. It had been decided that Dan would go back to York and take up his position as detective sergeant on this case, he was going to travel back with Jimmy Garner.

Chapter Six – Going Home

After an hour gathering up the paper work and making sure everything was signed in the right place and the correct forms had been filled in, the policemen set off for York. Jimmy Garner and Dan were the last to leave as they loaded up bags of evidence into the back of Jimmy's van.

Dan noted with a professional eye that although Jimmy was a ruddy faced jovial character he was good at his job. All the evidence had been bagged and tagged and then bagged again, even the paper suits and overshoes worn by everyone on the crime scene had been bagged and tagged. Dan carried the evidence bags down to the van while Jimmy loaded them. Jimmy had a clip board and as he loaded each bag he marked them off.

The back of the van was very well laid out and tidy. One side was racked with shelves, the top shelves held light everyday items boxes of latex gloves, over suits, and various sizes of plastic bags and containers, while the bottom shelves held black solid looking cases labelled with things like 'finger prints', 'Cameras' and 'Breathing Gear'. Welded to the forward bulkhead of the van that separated the driver from the cargo was a metal strong box locked and painted red, with a sign 'Danger Firearms'. Opposite the shelves hung an overcoat and a suit bag, Dan reckoned it must be a spare uniform, under them were a pair of trainers and a pair of wellies. The rest of the van was now full of evidence bags.

"I didn't think you were allowed to carry firearms without special permission" said Dan and nodded towards the yellow box, "Whey eye man no, I don't shoot 'em, it's for evidence I put guns, knives and drugs in there" replied Jimmy "I tell you what I could with some speed, I'm knackered. But I suppose a bottle of brown will have to do" said Jimmy.

Jimmy and Dan walked round to the front of the van "Hang on a minute" said Jimmy as he climbed into the cabin. Dan looked through the window and saw Jimmy clearing old sandwich wrappers, Macdonald's cartons and empty fag packets off the passenger seat, the cabin was full of crap. If the back of the van was first world then the cabin was definitely third world. "Ok, get in" said Jimmy as he opened the door, the smell of stale food and stale cigarettes hit Dan like a slap in the face, "I tell you what I'll go and get a bin bag from the pub" said Dan looking at the pile of rubbish in the foot well of the passenger seat.

When Dan returned with a black bag he found Jimmy sifting through the rubbish, it turned out not just to be old food wrappers but there were letters and receipts that Jimmy was collecting up and putting on one side. Dan filled the bin liner and then took it around the back of the pub looking for the bins. There he tried to open the doors to the out buildings, eventually he found a shed with the modern day collection of various coloured recycling bins. He looked through the gaps in the door to the out buildings next to the shed and saw enough gas bottles to blow the pub sky high and an enormous antiquated septic tank. Dan returned to the van and they finally set off for York.

Jimmy turned out to be nice a bloke and carried the conversation for most of the journey home. He gave Dan a quick run through of his life, told him some very funny but very dirty jokes and had a good moan about DI King, or as Jimmy called him 'Dick in'. Jimmy had walked a beat for ten years before becoming a SOCO. He freely admitted that he would never pass any of the fitness tests required of a policeman now, but he had been on all the courses the police could offer so while he was not the highest ranking SOCO in the force he was the most qualified, his fitness was why he hadn't had a promotion to sergeant. There was a collection of ready made of roll up cigarettes in the glove compartment and every 15 minutes Jimmy asked Dan if he minded if he smoked then lit up another roll-up, Dan was grateful for he loved the smell of fresh tobacco smoke and the ingrained smell of stale tobacco in the cabin was making him feel sick.

Jimmy was married with two children and whenever he could afford it took his son on 'pilgrimage' back to Newcastle to see the Toon Army. Jimmy's wife Liz worked in Tesco and could get a staff discount if Dan needed anything.

Dan had been dying to ask Jimmy a question and as they approached York's outer ring road he said "so what's with the van, I could perform surgery in the back and I'm gonna have tetanus booster after being up front for the last two hours", Jimmy shook his head and said "When I first became a SOCO I totally fucked up a case, there was some shite in the evidence bags and the paperwork was all wrong" for the first time in the nine hours Dan had known Jimmy he wasn't smiling. "This fella got off, and I had to go and see the deputy chief constable, luckily it was old Jonny, if it had been this woman we've got now, whey eye man, I'd've got the heave ho". "So what happened?" asked Dan. "That's why I've been on all the fuckin' courses" said Jimmy and laughed. Jimmy explained that he was naturally untidy, it was the only thing he and Liz argued about. After a disciplinary hearing when a case was dismissed from court due to the poor handling of evidence, Jimmy had attended several courses and had to hand in reports on his paperwork for nearly two years and now good practice was just habit.

Fell Walker by Peter Rankin © 2023

The drive through to the city centre even at night was one traffic jam after another, is was 9:30 and as they passed the bingo hall taxis waited in the rain to transport the purple rinses home. They approached Dan's flat on Gillygate or rather the basement flat of his mother's house. Dan thanked Jimmy for the lift and invited him in for a cuppa, but Jimmy wanted to be home before his children went to bed and so took a rain check.

Dan carried his bags down the narrow staircase in front of the house that lead to his front door. He unlocked the door and stepped in, it was dark and cold inside and didn't smell like home. Dan turned the light on there were stacks of boxes everywhere littering the floor and on top of his mum's old brown corduroy furniture. He put his put his bags down and opened the boxes one by one until he found the one he was looking for.

He pulled out an A4 diary the kind that has one day on each page, a stapler and a pencil. Dan went back over to his bags and emptied them out on the floor he took the photocopies of the statements everyone had made earlier the day and stapled them in the diary at today's date. Dan then sat down and spent the next three quarters of an hour writing down the events of yesterday and today in their relevant page in the diary. When he first joined the branch the CO of his first posting insisted that every case had it's own diary, a system Dan found so useful that every case Dan had worked had it's own diary, in his cellar at Robin Hood's Bay were boxes filled with old case diaries.

Dan washed his face in the kitchen sink and took one of his cookery books off the shelf, he flicked through the pages then went upstairs to his mum's flat. Dan had the basement, his mum let local groups use the ground floor as a meeting room they paid her what they could and she enjoyed the company, his mum had a flat on the first floor which he had never known to be empty of people and then on the second floor was another flat she rented out. Dan knocked on the door to her flat and the door swung open. "hi ya, it's me, I've told you about leaving that bloody door open" said Dan, Dan's mum ran across the room she was a blur of grey hair and tie dyed skirt and then threw herself at him, she tried to squeeze the life out of her son and Dan hugged her back now he knew he was home.

Mrs Margaret Cawood was 62, Dan never thought of her as an old woman she was still so active either socialising or helping out with another community project or another political campaign. Although she was a pensioner she was still an attractive woman and in her youth her good looks had got her out of many sticky situations. Dan always thought of his mum as the last of the hippies, she had never dyed her hair and had long grey almost white hair now nearly down to her waist and most of her clothes made you think she was on her way to a 60's fancy dress party.

"I don't need to lock the door there's policeman who lives down stairs" said Dan's mum as he put her down. "Look at you, you look like a Yeti" his mum said. "yeah I know, believe it or not I started work today" Dan said and then gave her a quick run down of the day's events. "Look mum I'm going for a curry do you want one?" Dan eventually asked "Oh yeah, vegetable byriannine and a naan, listen I've got a few people round they'll be gone by the time you get back, it'll be lovely to have a chat and don't forget my present".

"Frisky, get down" said Dan's mum, "look my favourite little girl happy to see my favourite little boy", there running around Dan's feet and chewing on his laces was a Yorkshire terrier tiny even for its breed. Dan liked that his mum had some company while he was away, but he knew sometime in the near future he would have to take it her for a walk, and look like total prat.

With everything that had happened Dan forgot about his mum's chocolates, ever since his first school trip when he was thirteen whenever Dan returned home he always brought a box of chocolates for his mum. Never mind he thought I'll get some from the Sainsbury local next to the curry house.

Fell Walker by Peter Rankin © 2023

Twenty minutes later Dan returned with a carrier bag full of curry, another one full of beer and a third with family size tin of quality street, Dan was told off for eating meat but then again he always was. After the curry he and his mother sat and laughed and chatted. By the time Dan headed off downstairs at 2am they had put the world to rights and his mum had promised to find Eva Longoria's phone number for him, as usual half way through her first bottle of lager his mum was happily pissed.

Once back in his flat Dan took his sleeping bag from the pile of belongings by the front door and laid it out on the living room floor, the only furniture he had were the brown corduroy chairs his mother had given him. Then he headed into the bathroom and stared at himself in the mirror, yesterday morning he looked rough but since then he'd found a body, met his new boss, started work, and had a session with his mum. Dan's eyes were red, his face looked totally wrung out and his hair and beard looked like a wire brush, to top it all he'd started to get wrinkles. Back in the living room Dan poured himself a whiskey, a dark peaty Islay single malt, his favourite and just another reason why he was skint. He let the whiskey roll around his tongue to get all the heady flavours, set his two alarm clocks for 5am and settled down to a fitful nights sleep on the floorboards.

Chapter Seven – Starting Over

Dan crawled out of his bed at 5am and straight into the bathroom, with his multicoloured head he didn't want to shave his whole head so he took out his clippers and cut his hair and beard back to an eighth of an inch. Then he went into the living room and emptied boxes on to the floor until he found some work clothes and an iron, the one part of his work Dan hated was wearing a suit. Dan put on his ironed check shirt, a pair of moleskin trousers, a tweed jacket and his old regimental tie, he looked every inch the country gentleman.

Dan looked around the flat, it looked like a squat that had been broken into. It hadn't been redecorated since the 1980s, the only furniture in the place belonged in a skip and his belongings were strewn across the floor. Dan looked around until he found his briefcase, it was a 1950s black leather ex treasury department one that he had bought in a junk shop years ago, it still had traces of where the silver portcullis was stamped on the closing strap.

From his bag Dan pulled out his laptop, a tiny Sony vaio he hadn't turned it on in over two weeks probably the longest time away from a computer in over ten years. Dan cleared his things off one of the chairs onto the floor sat down and turned the laptop on.

Dan connected to the internet, he had discovered that the hotel down the road had a wireless network for its' guests, their firewall was fairly simple to bypass and Dan had been getting free internet access at his mothers' house when he visited for the last 6 months. There were 45 e-mails in Dan's in box once he had deleted all the ones offering to either enlarge his penis or give him a credit card he was left with 16 e-mails that needed a reply. Dan got e-mails from all over the world from his friends in the army, Dan was on the reserve list and still retained his rank so they were addressed to Major Cawood. During the first Gulf War he had been one of the founder members of the 'AK47 Club', it was a group of junior security officers both US and British. The club still met once in a while mainly in war zones around the globe or at the funeral of a member, the last meeting had been in Afghanistan last year, when a group of now senior security officers, mercenaries, security consultants and one journalist met to drink, talk over old times and fire captured enemy AK47's.

Dan's e-mails had various pictures of serving US and British soldiers showing off their captured AK47s, a pang of jealousy ran through Dan. He'd loved being in the army and he'd seen enough front line action to know that the comedy in the e-mails he was receiving didn't hide the dangers his friends were currently in. Dan laughed out loud, the army's latest recruitment campaign had the slogan 'live the dream', a picture showing a troop of soldiers in an Afghan dessert appeared on screen they were all wearing t-shirts with the slogan 'we're living the dream'.

Dan's last e-mail was from the General, Dan's paternal grandfather had been a general in the US air force and even Dan's grandmother called him the General. Everything was alright on the ranch in Rhode Island and Dan wrote back telling the General about the events of the last two days. His grandfather always liked to hear about Dan's big cases he said it was better than reading Raymond Chandler.

Dan put on a pair of brown brogues, put his case diary, laptop, a military police regimental mug and a couple of tea bags into his briefcase grabbed his umbrella and headed off to work. It was only 7am but Dan was going to grab some breakfast on his walk to work, and because he forgot to ask yesterday he wasn't sure what time he was due to start.

After a McDonald's value meal a flick through the times and a twenty minute walk Dan found himself outside the North Yorkshire Police Headquarters, it was a nondescript big block of a 1970s building that was now starting to show its' age. Dan went through the smoked glass doors and into the surprisingly pokey reception with notice boards that held hundreds of out date leaflets and posters. He was met by Sergeant Ian

Fell Walker by Peter Rankin © 2023

Tompkins on reception and introduced himself, the desk sergeant sifted through a mountain of paperwork on the desk before finally phoning through to CID.

A police constable came through to reception and he and Dan were buzzed through the security doors into the police station proper. The inside of the station was a bit of a maze but Dan thought he could find his way back to reception. Dan was left in an empty CID office, it was a large open plan room with the door Dan had just walked through at one end and windows at the other, the side walls were lined with doors leading to offices for the DI's, conference rooms, file rooms and a small kitchen. The large centre room was the CID incident room it was full of desks in various states of disorder and any wall space without a window or door had either a notice board or white board.

Dan went into the little kitchen and looked through the cupboards until he found one full of mugs and put in his military police mug then put the kettle on. While he was waiting for the kettle to boil he wandered round the CID incident room looking at the different cases on different white boards. There was an indecent exposure, a series of burglaries, a couple of ASBOs, a conman working his way round all the hotels in the area and the murder of John Carter.

Dan sat down with a cup of tea and started on the sudoku in the times. At 8am DC Bush arrived, she introduced him to everyone and guided him around the office before showing him to his desk. Dan's desk was right outside DI King's office door.

DC Bush took Dan on a tour around the station finishing up in the admin office where she left him with the cryptic message "don't eat too much" Dan patted his belly and said "this is drink not food afraid", "No, I don't mean that just watch out for the DI he can be a bit of a bastard" with that DC Bush left leaving Dan none the wiser. Dan spent the next hour filling in forms, having his photo taken and being measured up for a new dress uniform.

Dan returned to the CID incident room to find DI King waiting for him, "It's nearly 10 I don't know how they do things in the Met but here we start work at 8:30" said the DI, "I got in at 8 I've been sorting out my paper work and warrant card, sir" said Dan. "Right then Danton you and me are gonna go for a ride so you'd better get your stuff".

DI King, DC Wheeler and Dan went down to the car pool and signed out a ford focus. Dan wondered where they were going but guessed that the DI was deliberately keeping him in the dark so didn't ask as he didn't want to give the man the satisfaction. They drove out of York and after about 20 minutes pulled into the car park of 'The Greasy Spoon' a road side café where all day breakfasts came in the three sizes normal, large and trucker. The three policemen went inside DC Wheeler and DI King both ordered a breakfast, Dan thought he'd better follow suit. He followed DC Bush's advice so only had a large all day breakfast. 'Well this is a good find' thought Dan as he ate his breakfast, while the other policemen laughed and joked.

"Right then Danton we've got an appointment with the Pathologist at twelve, I hope you're OK with dead bodies" Said DI King, "I've seen a couple during my time in the army" replied Dan, "Well we're about to get very personal with Mr John Carter" DI King said as he smiled at DC Wheeler. So this was the trick DC Bush tried to warn him about, DI King gave you a belly full of greasy food followed by a full autopsy, hoping to see his poor victim humiliated into being sick on the floor.

The first time Dan saw a dead body not made over by an undertaker was in the first Gulf War. Dan was part of the close protection group, providing security to high ranking officers and attached civilian personnel, the colonel he was driving went to see the front lines, they stopped to look at an Iraqi position that had been hit by a bomb. There was a trench filled with the mangled and charred remains of at least 20 men, they had been rotting in the dessert sun for half a day and both the colonel and young lieutenant Cawood stood by the trench and were sick until they had nothing left to be sick. Since then Dan had seen dead bodies in theatres of war across the globe.

Dan loved a good breakfast and a nice clean Y-Incision in a nice clean hospital wasn't about to part him from his black pudding. Every death he had investigated in 'The Branch' Dan had had to attend an autopsy and he never become blasé about dead bodies. At first he found it very difficult but Dan had come to see corpses as empty vessels, it was his coping mechanism. Jenny said that if he ever had therapy and this all came out Dan would end up wearing a white jumper with very long arms and living in a rubber room.

DC Wheeler drove DI King and Dan back into York and on to the district hospital. During the whole journey the pair of them told Dan horror stories about autopsies hoping to scare Dan out of even entering the hospital. Dan smiled and said nothing.

Once they were in the hospital DI King guided Dan to the morgue all the time continuing with gruesome autopsy stories. By now Dan had heard about someone who woke up in the middle of an autopsy, the Pathologist who accidentally cut off a policeman's fingers while he held the corpse's leg and the morgue attendant who didn't find death a barrier to love. Dan didn't tell the DI about the pregnant lance corporal he'd seen on the autopsy table, it was the worst thing he'd ever seen in his life and Dan hadn't eaten or slept for three days after that but drank an awful lot. In an anteroom of the autopsy suite the policemen washed, put on paper overalls a plastic apron, a pair of white wellies and a clear plastic visor.

The DI and Dan went into the autopsy room, Dan was hit by the smell of raw lamb just like all corpses "Well Major Cawood, what the bloody hell are you doing in my morgue!" came a voice from the other side of John Carter. Dan looked behind the blood spattered visor of the pathologist there was a pair of friendly eyes. Dan walked quickly across the room and gave the pathologist a big hug that lifted her clean off her feet.

The Pathologist was emeritus Professor of pathology Beatrice Gerry or Bea to her friends, she was in her early fifties and although she was only five foot dead she was a very robust woman and spoke with a 1950s BBC accent. Bea had worked with the Met on some of their most difficult cases in the last twenty years and was a civilian consultant to the MoD, but most importantly of all she was Dan's friend.

Dan put Bea down and said "It's DS Cawood now , and this is DI King", "DI King I've met, but it's not very often I get to meet people I like in here, not living anyway. This is my assistant David" replied Bea as she pointed to the only other man in the room. It turned out that Bea's husband who was a sculptor had received a lottery grant to open the North Yorkshire Sculpture Park and with the children having left home the Gerrie's moved to York to start a new life. "I retired, but I couldn't stand being at home all day and I was driving Tim mad. The job of Chief Pathologist came up here and I still do a spot of lecturing" Bea told Dan.

Bea had started the autopsy, she had made the Y-Incision, a deep cut in the shape of a Y from both shoulders down to the breast bone and then a single straight line down past the navel. The cut went right through to the bone and the flap of skin from John Carter's chest was folded back and now covered his face. The autopsy was well under way Bea had removed the heart and lungs and the organs of the trunk were just being taken out, and David had just cut off the top of the corpses head and was removing the brain.

"So Major what do you see?" said Bea as she struggled with John Carter's liver, it was a game they had played ever since he had brought her a corpse eight years ago in London. "I actually found the body and he had blue lips and finger tips and petecchial haemorrhaging of the eyes, so I guess suffocation" Dan said as he lifted the eye lids of the corpse. "Very good Cawood, as a reward I shall borrow your little cottage for a week, my granddaughter is coming to see me next half term" said Bea "He was healthy and big hearted as it turned out" Bea carried on as she pointed to a heart in a stainless steel bowl on the trolley. "That's a whopper" said Dan, "I know would you mind finding its' capacity for me, there are some measuring cylinders in that cupboard over there behind David".

Dan filled John Carters heart with water while DI King held veins and arteries closed he didn't look very happy. "Will this establish cause of death" asked DI King, "Oh, no but it's jolly interesting don't you think" replied Bea, with that DI King dropped the heart into the sink and wiped his hands on Dan's paper overalls. Dan could tell this wasn't going quite how the DI had planned. "when will your report be ready doctor?" asked the DI, "Oh, pop on through to my office, I'll only be five minutes and David can finish here" replied Bea.

Dan and the DI went through to Bea's office and sat in silence. The autopsy suite and Bea's office were both well decorated and seemed to have modern up to date equipment. Bea had once told Dan she could order whatever she fancied for the morgue because if a bean counter questioned her spending plans then they might have to come down here and see for themselves what was needed, and if you don't have to, no-one wants to go into an autopsy suite.

After five minutes Bea came in and pulled off her gloves and paper overalls, "well inspector your Mr Carter died from oxygen starvation to the brain. He had no defensive wounds and didn't appear to put up a fight and I found two small white feathers lodged in his trachea. I can't say anything else for certain until the tox screens come back, but I would guess and this is only a guess mind you and won't go in my final report he was suffocated with a pillow in his sleep" she said as she sat down behind her desk. "What sort of feathers were they doctor?" enquired the DI, "I'm strictly humans I'm afraid, now the Major maybe able to help you there he's a regular Ray Mears" said Bea, DI King was looking unhappier and unhappier.

Tea and coffee arrived and they remained in Bea's office for the next half hour going over the minutia of John Carters physical condition. Even though smoking wasn't allowed in the hospital Bea smoked her pipe through the whole meeting, Dan thought it would be a brave administrator who took on Professor Gerry in her own back yard, he had seen her in full flight and was just glad she was on his side.

DI King excused himself and went to the toilet, Bea came round to Dan's side of the desk and sat on the edge of it. "I was desperately sorry to hear about your divorce" said Bea as she reached out and grabbed Dan's shoulder, "but I'm bloody glad to see a friendly face". Dan felt exactly the same way.

Bea invited Dan for supper later in the week, he knew that meant a little food followed by smoking, drinking and talking into the wee small hours. Supper at the Gerries was always an interesting occasion she knew everyone who was anyone in the legal and medical professions and Tim knew everyone in the arts, he had taught most of them at the Slade school of fine art.

DI King came back into the office, Bea promised to have her final report on the DI's desk as soon as possible, but she thought her preliminary findings wouldn't change. Dan and the DI left the hospital with John Carters clothes and a little plastic bag containing two small white feathers. Dan knew the feathers were from an eider duck which meant they came from an expensive pillow, he thought he would keep that to himself he'd pissed off the DI enough for one day.

They found DC Wheeler outside the hospital parked in a disabled parking space sat on the bonnet of the car smoking a cigarette with his mobile phone stuck to his ear. DC Wheeler put the phone away and said "right gov, where to next?" "You're never gonna believe this but young Danton here knows Dame Death" said DI King and then carried on with his best posh accent "and later in the week he's going to pop round for supper". Dan was getting pig sick of DI King but he wasn't about to rise to the bait, DI King was his superior officer, Dan knew he had to leave the force or just take it. Hopefully if Dan didn't react the DI would get bored and go back to one of his normal victims in a couple of days.

"Right then back to the nick, I think we need to find Mrs Carter" said DI King and with that the three policemen drove back to the police HQ. It was another quiet journey for Dan while DI King and DC Wheeler took the Mickey out of other officers. After a morning in DI King's and DC Wheeler's company Dan felt he knew all the station gossip.

Once back at the station DI King contacted the Cumbria Constabulary and a photo of Mrs Carter was faxed through within minutes, Dan confirmed she was the same redhead who just two days earlier had thrown a holdall full of rags at John Carter. DI King contacted the Crown Prosecution Service, Dan was in the office.

Personally Dan thought the man was a wanker, but he understood why he was a DI, he explained what had happened in the last 48 hours, the argument in the pub, the murder, the red hairs at the scene and the whereabouts of Mrs Carter. Dan was impressed he was very slick and wanted a quick arrest and within half an hour an arrest warrant was made out in the name of Judith Carter.

The rest of the day was spent filling out forms and writing reports for the CPS. Dan sat at his desk and typed away, after about half an hour DI King whistled at him, Dan looked round to see the DI waving his mug in the air. "I'd love one thanks sir, tea strong and milky with no sugar" said Dan and returned to his work. Dan didn't look up but he knew the DI would be seething, after about a minute he whistled again and snapped his fingers but Dan carried on ignoring him. Eventually DI King walked over to Dan's desk and said "in my office now".

DI King closed his office door behind Dan, sat down leaving Dan standing and said "Right fuckwit lets get one thing straight, I'm the governor round here and when I say jump you say how high? Got it Danton" "Yes sir" Dan had been long enough in the army to know that the answer to every question was 'yes sir'. "So what's your fuckin' problem" said the DI, "I've got no problem sir" Dan replied with dumb insolence. "Well why won't you answer my fuckin' call" said the DI, "I'm sorry sir, I mustn't have heard you" still with dumb insolence. "You fuckin' heard alright, everyone in the fuckin' incident room heard" the DI shouted. "I'm sorry sir, I didn't hear you call my name" still dumb insolence, still calm and quiet. The DI clicked his fingers and said "that is you Sergeant", Dan waited a couple of seconds and said "Whistles and clicks are for dogs sir, I believe my proper address is Detective Sergeant Cawood". If anyone in Dan's command in the army had talked to him the way he was talking to the DI, Dan would have had him for breakfast. But if Dan had treated anyone in his command the way DI King treated his officers he would have been out on his ear.

"Right then Detective Sergeant Cawood I would like a cup of coffee, now" said the DI this time he was calm but tried to put menace in his voice. After a few seconds wait Dan replied "very good sir, I'll be back presently".

Dan left the DI's office and headed to the kitchenette, everyone in the incident room was silent and staring at him. Dan had a good look through all the cupboards but couldn't find what he was looking for so left the incident room. He returned five minutes later to a still silence room and headed back into the kitchenette. DC Bush walked into the kitchen behind him and whispered "Where the hell have you been, the DI's fuming". Dan smiled and waved a cup and saucer in the air "the man ordered a cup of coffee and a cup of coffee is what he' going to get" said Dan.

A few minutes later Dan knocked on the DI's door, "come" said the DI, Dan went in and put the cup and saucer on the desk "one cup of coffee as ordered, sir" Dan said then stared into the cup, "what's wrong with you?" snapped the DI, "it's nothing sir, I just thought I saw a hair" Dan said and walked out of the room.

With all the paperwork finished Dan walked home at six o'clock, he'd had easier days on active service and with a lot less dangerous enemies. On his way home he stopped off at marks and sparks and bought some fresh tuna.

Once home Dan found the packing case he was looking for took out some cooking essentials put on some heavy rock music and made himself sushi. Dan loved to cook he found it relaxing, he sang his heart out to AC/DC as made the maki rolls.

Once he'd eaten and had a glass of whisky and a pipe of tabacco Dan sat down and wrote in his case diary the events of the day. Then he e-mailed Bea to get directions to her new house and finally Dan put on a film and crawled into his sleeping bag on the floor and fell asleep watching The Shawshank Redemption.

Chapter Eight – A grand day out

Dan woke at 5:30 and had sushi for breakfast washed down with a cup of tea, all the time he could hear the constant yapping of a small dog. Dan went upstairs to his mother's flat to find the door open and Frisky running round having a mad half hour. Dan found a lead and the nappy sacks and took the dog out for a walk.

Dan walked down to the river just 5 minutes away, the sun had been up for an hour or so but it was still quite chilly. Dan loved York in the very early morning, it was still small enough not to be a 24hour city and he found he was walking streets alone that in just two would be gridlocked. The early morning sun reflected off the river and Dan could see the Minster and the City walls in the distance.

Dan looked at his watch it was 6:15am, just 48 hours earlier John Carter had been murdered in his sleep, it felt like weeks ago. Dan walked further along the river bank, the footpath opened out into an open field. In only fifteen minutes he was almost in open country walking on Clifton Ings the natural flood plain to the river Ouse. The river flooded so often that there had never been any development on the river banks and it meant that even in the city centre of York you were never more than a 15 minutes walk from some fresh air and open space. Some teenagers had camped out by the river they were sat outside their tent shivering and smoking. Frisky ran straight up to them looking for affection, Dan walked over and asked "Peaceful night?" "No we had all the drunks coming back from the pub at midnight and then someone woke us up riding their mini-motor bike round the Ings about half an hour ago". Dan chatted for a while and then took Frisky home.

Once home Dan packed an overnight bag with a clean set of work clothes, a pair of shoes, and a wash kit, in a job like Dan's you never know when clean clothes will come in handy. Then he put on his work clothes grabbed the overnight bag and walked to the station, again he was the first in the incident room arriving before 8. DC Bush arrived a few minutes later and brought her chair over to Dan's desk for a chat. "So you pissed the DI off yesterday" she said "yeah I think so, does he always behave like that?" replied Dan, "only when he needs to show people who's boss, he can be very nice when he wants to be or should I say has to be" said DC Bush.

"So does everyone call you Bushy" asked Dan, "no just the DI, I'm Naz to my friends", Dan wasn't surprised to hear that the DI had a nickname for everyone. Dan and Naz were getting on like a house on fire when the DI arrived bang on 8:30.

Fell Walker by Peter Rankin © 2023

"I'm glad to see you two are getting on well, I've got a little job for you to do" said DI King as he walked through the incident room to his office. "Oh bloody hell this sounds like a long day" said Naz and with that she and Dan followed the DI into his office. "Right then you two, I've been on to the Cumbria force this morning and they are expecting you later on today to pick up Mrs Carter" said DI King with a smile on his face and carried on "then when she gets here I think me and you we'll get her straight into interrogation Danton". Dan tallied up the day in his head at least a three and a half hour drive to Carlisle then paperwork followed by the same journey and more paperwork and finally what could be hours in an interview room.

Naz went down to the motor pool to sign out a car while the DI sorted out the paperwork needed to transfer Mrs Carter from Cumbria to North Yorkshire. Dan stayed in the DI's office "well Danton what is it?" asked the DI. "I'd like permission to stop at the school Mr and Mrs Carter worked at and ask the headmaster a few questions. I spoke informally to some of his students the other day and I feel there's more to this than meets the eye" said Dan. "Very well you're only wasting your own time." Said the DI then leant back and stretched in his chair as if to show Dan what a relaxing day he was about to have.

Fell Walker by Peter Rankin © 2023

By the time the car was ready, paperwork sorted out, a meeting arranged with the headmaster of Keswick High School and provisions bought for the journey it was 10:30.

Dan pulled out of the motor pool and set off to the lakes. It was a journey he knew well, as a younger man he had enjoyed many weekends under canvas in either the Dales or the Lakes. Dan and Naz chatted which meant that Naz talked and Dan listened. He found out a lot.

The DI had arrived from Thames Valley 6 years ago as a DS and had the reputation of being a bit of a bastard. The then DI was retired due to ill health and DS King was made acting DI. During his time as acting DI the police work was crap but he made sure that all the paper work was done properly and up to date for any outstanding cases, so for a couple of months the crime figures looked great because it looked like he had solved loads of cases in just a couple of weeks. Everyone who worked for him thought he was a wanker, but because he could put on the charm when he wanted to and always had his paperwork up to date the bean counters upstairs loved him.

Dan listened to the station gossip and Naz was just confirming what he had heard from the DI and DC Wheeler yesterday. Everyone thought the new uniform PC was gay, Sergeant Tompkins was getting a divorce after his wife found out about him and the girl from the CCTV unit and the big rumour was the station was getting shut down along with the Harrogate station to be replaced with a new constabulary HQ on a green field site which would mean redundancies.

Finally after a quick stop for a cuppa in Ingleton Naz gave Dan her life story for the rest of the journey. Her mother was from London and her father was Iranian, he had moved to the UK after the Shah of Iran was overthrown in 1979. Her parents still lived in London's fashionable West End, but she thought of herself as having moved out of home when she was sent to boarding school at the age of 11. Naz had studied law at Newcastle University and had joined the Police on their fast track scheme for graduates, she had only been in the force for 2 years and had already sat and passed her sergeant's exams. She was in love and had just married Ian Bush a human rights solicitor working in Leeds who she met at University, the two of them were renovating a Barn just outside Harrogate and living on site in a static caravan. Ian wanted children right now but Naz wanted to build her dream house and get her career started first.

Dan had listened to Naz for hours she had a pleasant voice and it was nice just being in the presence of a pretty woman. He knew her whole life story and yet she knew nothing about him. Dan didn't know it but he made it very easy for people to trust him, a skill that made him a fantastic interrogator. He had very strong morals and almost never lied, a result of being brought up by his mother. This of course meant his mouth would often get him into trouble, which was why he was just starting a 14 hour day.

Dan pulled into the Car Park of Keswick community college and Tertiary education centre and put his tie back on. He and Naz got out of the car and made their way through a sea of school children moving between lessons as the two of them headed towards reception. The school was a typical comprehensive built during the early 1960's to educate the baby boomers and extended regularly since then to make a hotchpotch ugly looking building in varying states of decay. Once into the building it was obvious the entire repair budget of the school had been spent on the reception. It was spread over two floors with fancy lights, plasma screens and a fish tank. Dan smiled and whispered "you can't polish shite".

"Good afternoon we've got an appointment with the headmaster, this is DS Cawood and I'm DC Bush" said Naz as she showed the receptionist her warrant card and Dan her annoyed face. They were quickly ushered through to the heads office suite and offered a drink. Within moments the head appeared and took them into his study "This is a black time for the school and many of our children have been very upset in the last few days. I would appreciate it if we could keep your presence here as low key as possible" said the head. "Of course, we understand it must be a very difficult time especially as nothing is yet certain" said Dan, "Oh I thought it was an open and shut case haven't you arrested Mrs Carter" said the head. "We are holding someone in connection with the case and they are helping with our enquiries, but we are still waiting on the coroner to pronounce the cause of death" Dan said with his best poker face, "Oh I understand, now what can I do for you?" replied the head with a smile.

"I understand from the pupils that were with Mr Carter at the Lion Inn that his employment record was less than exemplary, I realise you don't want to speak ill of the dead but other peoples lives are in the balance" said Dan, "I was new to the school last year and as you say there was an incident which all revolved around his daughter's pregnancy. It was all resolved at the time and the parents of the boy who Mr Carter allegedly hit didn't want to take the matter any further, so I gave all concerned some time off school as a chance to reflect" said the head.

"Is there anyone in school who has been here long enough to remember Mr Carter arriving?" asked Dan "Colin Jackson the head of sixth form has been here longer than anyone he maybe able to help you" said the head. With that the he phoned through to his secretary to bring Colin through to the head's study.

Colin Jackson was a tall happy looking man in his early fifties, he had been at the school since leaving teacher training college at the age of 21. He said proudly that he had seen out 4 headmasters and two changes of school name and with a big grin that he would see out another one of each before his retirement.

Colin could remember John Carter arriving over twenty years earlier the school was then a small secondary modern just serving the town of Keswick, not the sprawling community college it was today. Everyone knew everyone and the school was at the heart of the community. John Carter was one of the students' favourites he ran the woodworking department back when there was one and gave up lots of time to help the pupils after school. Even when they had left school pupils use to come and see him. There was a rumour that he was more than friendly with one of his ex-pupils but then he got married and nothing further was said about it. "It all came to a head when this lad Davy James gassed himself because he had a big crush on John. There was a big enquiry, John was really upset and there were a whole load of things that came out in the wash. Stuff that you'd just get sacked for nowadays but they were different times back then.

John could be a bit of a bugger but his downfalls were the barmaids at The Fox not little boys" said Colin.

Dan and Naz thanked the head for his time and got back on the road. "I don't like what I hear about John Carter" said Naz as they drove toward Carlisle, "no, this isn't as clean cut as the DI thinks" said Dan. They talked about the case and what had happened in the Lion Inn for the rest of the journey, there was something about the whole case that had been troubling Dan since this morning but he couldn't put his finger on it.

On arrival at Carlisle police station Dan and Naz took the opportunity to grab a bite to eat. Dan loved police canteens you could always get a fried breakfast and a mug of industrial strength tea. After a good feed Dan left Naz in the canteen with a whole new set of admirers, while he headed off to sort out the paperwork on Mrs Carter.

It took Dan over an hour getting the correct signatures and stamps on his paperwork before he and Naz were finally back on the road. Naz drove on the way home and Dan sat in the back next to Mrs. Carter just the way it was written in the police manual. The trip to Carlisle had been quite jovial but the journey back was silent and depressing.

Fell Walker by Peter Rankin © 2023

Just outside Skipton about halfway home Mrs Carter asked if she could have a cigarette. Dan had spent the last hour and a half studying her and she was a nervous wreck, if she wasn't staring at nothing she was crying if she wasn't crying she was chewing her nails and pulling her hairs out one by one. Dan could remember a greasy spoon in a lay by about 5 miles ahead and if it was still there they could stop for a smoke and a cup of tea. He looked in the rear view mirror he could see Naz staring at him and mouthing the word no. It was against procedure but Mrs. Carter wasn't going anywhere.

Once in the lay by Naz got the teas and Dan and Mrs. Carter got out of the car for a smoke. "I love the smell of a pipe, it reminds me of my granddad" said Judith Carter, it was the first time he'd seen her smile, and she could be quite pretty. "It's part of my 10 year quitting smoking plan" Dan said as he blew out a large cloud of purple smoke.

"Have we met before" asked Judith, "I was staying in the Lion Inn the night your husband died" said Dan. "Oh" she replied and sucked hard on her cigarette. "I didn't do it you know" Judith said after a brief pause. "Well we haven't heard all the facts yet" said Dan and then Naz turned up with the teas.

Naz still didn't look happy, stopping for a cuppa was strictly against procedure and if anything happened Dan was in deep trouble, but he thought it was the human thing to do. They drank Tea and began to chat even Naz lightened up, by the time they had been on the road 10 minutes Naz was describing what her new en-suite would look like.

It had gone 8pm by the time they drove into the station and Naz and Dan took Judith Carter through to the cells, she was processed by the duty sergeant and was to see the police doctor to make sure she was fit for an interview. Only Naz was allowed in with the doctor so Dan went off to get a wash, whenever he travelled he felt dirty.

After his wash Dan phoned DI King to tell him they had arrived, and then got in touch with the duty solicitor to be ready to come in, just in case Judith Carter wanted legal representation.

Chapter Nine – A little Chat

Dan sat in the darkened incident room and waited for DI King, the next thing he knew the DI was shaking him and saying "wakey wakey Danton, time for an interview" once Dan had come round he then shouted "get on your fuckin' feet and get yourself down to the interview rooms" and with that the DI walked out. Dan wiped his own dribble off his shirt, splashed some water on his face and went down stairs.

The DI was waiting outside interview room 1 he was well groomed as always and made a point of waiting for Dan. "Right then Cawood I want you to read the defendant her rights, explain about the tape and ask about legal representation. Basically I want you to deal with procedure, I'll do the questioning. If I need some thinking time I'll put both elbows on the table so that's when I'd like you to ask a question any question I'm not bothered what, but just one if there's any follow up I'll do it. Got it?" Dan nodded and they went into the interview room.

Dan did as he was asked and read Judith Carter her rights then explained the interview procedure. She didn't want legal representation so the DI got stuck in. Despite himself Dan liked the DI's style it was totally opposite to his own. Where Dan got personal and emotional, the DI stayed remote and objective. "In your own words describe the events of the night of your husband's death" said the DI, Judith Carter replied while the DI took notes.

"I was at home when my husband's mobile phone began to ring, he should have had it with him as he was on a school trip. Normally I wouldn't have answered it but he was the emergency contact for the trip so I answered it, it was a text message from one of his pupils called Justin thanking him for a lovely day. John has a history with his pupils grooming one to be his special friend, it's nothing sexual honestly but they often get the wrong idea. Once John had to turn down a member what he called his club's sexual advances the lad was so distressed he committed suicide. I told John then I wasn't putting up with it any more and before we got married he promised to stop it and close down his after school club. There was a real who-ha in the school when that lad died John nearly lost his job. So when I saw the text message I thought it was happening all over again and just saw red. I went upstairs got all his clothes 'cos he loved his clothes, cut them all up shoved them in a bag, grabbed a bottle of vodka and drove to that bloody pub in the middle of nowhere. Once I got there I had a bit of a rant and threw his clothes at him then drove off. I drove into a village called Rosedale parked the car up near an old ruin and got drunk."

"and what happened the following morning?" said the DI. "I woke up at 6am clutching the empty bottle of vodka and wrapped in a blanket on a park bench with a thumping head. I walked around the valley for an hour or so with the biggest hangover, then got in my car and drove home I cried all the way. I probably shouldn't have been driving I was still over the limit. I got home just after twelve and Chris Redman one of the deputy head's was waiting outside in his car, he told me what had happened to John and I asked him to leave. I went into the house to sit down and cry and then the police arrived they asked me where I'd been the night before, after they left I gave the kids a load of money to order pizza and drank John's expensive whisky and went to sleep drunk".

DI King looked at his notes and began to ask questions in quick fire succession "where is this mobile phone now?", "do you often see red?", "how often do you normally go to bed drunk?", "How did you feel cutting up his clothes?" Judith Carter answered them all but was beginning to sound unsteady.

There was a knock on the door a PC entered put a slip of paper in front of the DI and left, the DI put both elbows on the table and read the note. "You must have driven for hours to get to the pub and yet when you arrived you were still to use your words 'seeing red' is it common for you to remain very angry for such a long period" said Dan, "No" said Judith Carter and burst in to tears.

"Apart from the public bar did you enter any other room in the hotel?" asked the DI, "No" said Judith through her tears. "There were a number of red hairs in your husband's hotel room that match yours for colour, would you be willing to give DNA sample to rule yourself out?" The DI followed up quickly while Judith shook and murmured "yes". "The tread pattern of one of your shoes matches that found on the pillow we believe killed your husband, can you explain that?" said the DI with a look that said 'game over' and put his elbows back on the table. Judith just cried as Dan asked "are you sure you don't require legal representation?", again just tears.

The interview was suspended and the duty solicitor called, by the time she arrived it was 10:30pm the same questions were asked with the same answers given. It wasn't looking good for Judith Carter but there was something niggling Dan and he couldn't put his finger on it. When all the paperwork was done it was so late it was almost early the DI had a huge grin on his face and Dan could understand why, a murder case cracked in 48 hours that looked pretty bloody good. "It's been a long and productive day Danton, you can have tomorrow morning off" said the DI as he left the station.

Fell Walker by Peter Rankin © 2023

As Dan walked home even the kebab shops were closed, he was absolutely knackered. He finally got home wrote up his case diary and fell into his sleeping bag with a glass of whisky. He tossed and turned all night sleeping fitfully, every time he awoke he couldn't put his finger on it but something was wrong.

Chapter ten – The Boss

Dan finally got out of bed at 10:30, he showered, checked his e-mails and set off for work. On his walk to work he stopped at the burger van in the open air market and got a cheeseburger for breakfast.

Dan got into the incident room just before midday, there was a bit of a party atmosphere and everyone looked happy. Dan walked over to Naz's desk and asked "What's happening?" "The CPS are going to prosecute Judith Carter for the murder of her husband, the DI has broken the station record for solving a murder case" said Naz. "Maybe he'll be in a better mood today then" said Dan "Oh yeah he's buying a drink for anyone in the pub at 6 tonight, if he's getting his wallet out he must be happy" said Naz.

Dan sat at his desk and checked his messages, there was one from the chief superintendent inviting him for coffee and a chat at 11am this morning "opps" said Dan to himself and phoned her secretary to apologise.

Within minutes Dan found himself waiting outside Stella Davis's office, the chief superintendent had a reputation of being a tough, hard, career copper. Dan was kept waiting for over an hour, eventually she appeared out of her office and said "I'm sorry to keep you but I believe we did have an appointment earlier this morning".

Stella Davis was responsible for the York region of the North Yorkshire police, she was a stout woman with white hair and spoke with a posh Yorkshire accent, she was either trying to hide her roots or came from a rich background. Stella smiled with a smile that said beware and said "DS Cawood would you like to come into my office".

Her office was very nice, modern looking and functional, there was no sign of a person behind the uniform, no photograph on the desk, no personal knick-knacks around the room. Dan explained why he missed his appointment earlier in the day Stella Davis didn't seem impressed.

The chief superintendent told Dan how she ran a tight ship with targets met and paperwork done and new initiatives taken on, she wasn't happy about taking on a new DS she knew nothing about and waved Dan's flimsy personnel file in the air. "So Sergeant you need to impress me, what did you do in the army?" asked Stella.

Dan spent the next half hour talking, he took Stella Davis on a brief tour of his career in the army. Dan started out as an infantry officer with the Prince of Wales own Yorkshire regiment, he was recruited by the Military Police just out of Sandhurst for an undercover operation. After that he transferred to the Royal Military Police and did close protection work during the first Gulf War and his first tour of Northern Ireland at the height of the troubles. He was promoted to Captain and sent to London to join 'The Branch' the special investigation branch of the Military Police, during his time in London he liaised with other national security organisations and worked on a number of high profile cases. Dan was transferred to Gibraltar to be a security adviser to the chief minister and to take command of the Military Police on the Island, it was on Gibraltar Dan learnt to speak Spanish. On his return to London he was promoted Major and spent the next last few years of his career based in London but flying into war zones as a security and police adviser, these included Kosovo, the second Gulf War and Afghanistan. Afghanistan was his last posting, it was there he was wounded in action for the second time and received the Military Cross for bravery.

Stella Davis listened dispassionately with a poker face and when Dan had finished said "Such a glittering career, why did you leave?" Dan explained that his wife was unhappy with his constant absence from home and because he loved her he resigned his commission. "So why did you leave the Met?" asked Stella Davis. Dan explained that his wife was unhappy with his constant presence at home and because she no longer loved him, he decided to move back home to York.

Fell Walker by Peter Rankin © 2023

Stella Davis spent the next fifteen minutes telling Dan what was expected of him in the North Yorkshire Service and with that he was dismissed. On his way out of the door Stella Davis said "Oh by the way Cawood do you shoot?" Dan thought about the questioned and replied "not as sport Marm, but I was trained as an infantry officer and to use small arms as a member of the close protection squad" Dan was about to leave and then added "and I'm a crack shot".

Dan went down to the canteen and settled in front of a full English, by the time he returned to the incident room the place was a ghost town with just a few people working. When Dan asked he found that most people had left just minutes earlier at four o'clock and gone down to the local pub to celebrate with the DI.

Dan finished off the paperwork that was left over from the last few days checked there was no new messages from Stella Davis and went to the pub for a pint.

Once there Dan found the place full of coppers he only meant to stay for a couple, but sat down with Naz and a couple of her friends from uniform and before he knew it, it was late and Naz's husband had joined them for a drink.

Ian Bush was slim and of medium height, he wasn't some much handsome but pretty and spoke with south London accent. Dan wasn't sure what to make of him but as the night flowed on he found a kindred spirit who enjoyed a good joke and a pint of beer. At about 10 the DI came over to speak to them he was plastered, Dan congratulated the DI on his success and hoped he wouldn't remember it in the morning.

When the pub shut everyone got taxis into town some of them to a nightclub, but Dan followed his stomach and went with a group to a curry house. A long wait, Popadoms, naan bread, Rogan Josh, Lager and laughter followed. Dan then walked out of the curry house propping up the staggering Bushes. Dan wasn't drunk he was happy, he was a big bloke and it took a lot to get him pissed.

The Bushes and Dan made their way back to Dan's tiny flat, Dan went upstairs and made up a bed on one of the sofas in his mum's community room. He put the bushes to bed and went downstairs wrote his case diary the best he could and fell asleep in the chair.

Fell Walker by Peter Rankin © 2023

Chapter Eleven – Party Time

Dan was woken by his mother at 8am "There's a couple upstairs, I don't think they're anything to with me" said Dan's mum with some uncertainty. "It's alright mum they're not one of your waifs and strays, it's DC Bush and her husband Ian" said Dan as he tried to work out where he was, "I can't believe you've got bloody coppers sleeping in my house" Dan's mum whispered. "How many times mother, I'm one of your fascist bully boy establishment types, and it was fascist establishment money that bought you this bloody house" Dan said as he rubbed his temples and felt his back, a night on a chair meant he could hardly move. The house on Gillygate had been a wedding present from 'The General' to Dan's parents back in the 60s.

"Mum they're really nice, just go and talk to them" Dan said as his mum walked out of the door. Dan got up brushed the fur off his teeth and had a shower long shower he put on a pair of shorts, tee-shirt and a pair of sandals and went upstairs. He found his mum sat on the end of the sofa that the Bushes were lying on, all three of them were drinking tea and Dan's mum was telling them embarrassing stories of Dan's youth.

"Does anyone fancy hunting down a full English?" said Dan, "Yeah if there a vegetarian option" said Ian. "Did you know Ian's a human right's solicitor, he's going to have a look the Mishra's case for me" said Dan's mum, "the who?" said Dan, "you know the friends of Mr Woo who are seeking asylum" said Dan's mum, then she left to go back upstairs mouthing 'they're really nice'.

Dan and the Bushes went over the road from the house there was a lovely little bistro café, they sat and ate a full English breakfast then read the morning papers. Together they finished the times jumbo crossword while drinking tea and coffee, it was how Dan loved to spend mornings. Naz loved the décor and asked the manager where they got the floor tiles from, she thought they would look lovely in their new hallway. The Bushes set off for home and Dan went into town to buy a bed.

Once Dan had spent money he didn't have on furniture he didn't want, he wandered back to his flat and read through the case diary of John Carter's murder. The case was closed, but Dan was still unhappy about something and he couldn't put his finger on it. Dan checked his e-mails a few messages from the AK47 club and one from 'the General'.

Dan phoned his cottage in Robin Hood's Bay "Hi there, what do you think of the place" Dan said when the phone was answered "Man this place is crazy" said Josh. Dan had let Josh have the keys to his cottage when he left the Lion Inn a few days ago. Dan knew he wouldn't have time to see Josh and the other walkers with the murder case and thought his American friend deserved a bit of luxury. Dan told Josh where there was an emergency £20 note between the pages of a book on the shelves in the living room and told him to go and get a good feed at the Dolphin Inn. Josh thought the Bay was great, it was full of characters and the views from the cottage were amazing. Josh was going to spend a few more days around the Bay and was coming to see Dan next weekend in York.

Dan opened another one of his packing cases and found his helmet, leather jacket and trousers. He packed his camping gear in a rucksack and put on his finest Hawaiian Shirt a lovely original 1960s light brown shirt with great big yellow flowers, Dan had found it on a market stall years ago in Petticoat Lane. Dan threw his camping gear and toothbrush in a bag and went out the back of the house and pulled the plastic sheet off his shiny black triumph triple. It was his pride and joy the motorbike of his dreams, Dan loved the classic English styling combined with the reliability of a modern bike. He pulled out of the back yard and set off for Bea's way too fast.

It took Dan about three hours to do the 45 minute ride to Bea's house, she lived near Malton and Dan couldn't resist riding round the Howardian Hills that surrounded Castle Howard then up on to the North

Yorkshire Moors where only Days earlier John Carter had been murdered. By the time he got to Bea's he was sweaty but happy.

Bea had a beautiful home in a village just outside Malton, it would have been the manor house years ago. It was a lovely Georgian building with a cottage and granary surrounded by formal gardens and paddocks, Naz could easily pick up a few ideas thought Dan. He parked his bike on the Gravel drive amongst all the cars and erected his bivvy-bag on the lawn, a one man tent no bigger than a coffin, he took off his leathers put on his shorts and walked over to the big house for supper.

Dan rang the bell and after a few moments an ebullient Bea opened the door and pulled Dan into the house "Major it's always lovely to see you and I know Tim will adore the shirt" and with that he was given a big hug. "I've camped on your lawn I hope you don't mind I thought I'd have a few beers" said Dan, "my dear Major there's just the two of us rattling round in this big old pile, I insist you have a room" said Bea.

Bea took Dan from the porch into the hall and it soon became apparent that supper was a packed house with nearly everyone in evening dress, there was even the odd dress uniform and Dan realised these people were the movers and shakers in North Yorkshire. Dan looked round and saw Tim wearing a bright yellow matching caftan and hat he was talking to some people that were obviously artists one them was wearing a bright purple velvet dinner jacket and tie. Dan smiled to himself it was always a fun night at Bea's.

Dan was introduced to everyone as "Major Cawood MC" as he was ushered through the house by Bea and into the kitchen. It was a lovely big farmhouse kitchen with staff from the catering company running round making sure no-one went hungry or thirsty. "Is everything OK?" said the catering manager slightly worried "Oh yes, marvellous" replied Bea.

"Now then Major I've got a treat for you" said Bea as she reached into a cupboard and pulled out a bottle of whisky. It was a 30 year old Islay single malt, Bea and Dan went out into the garden smoked their pipes and savoured their whisky while they put the world to rights. Half an hour later Bea apologised for leaving Dan but she had to attend to her other guests and poured Dan another large whisky before heading back inside.

Dan rejoined the party he got chatting to a few people and Bea came over with a man in his early fifties wearing the dress uniform of a colonel. He was Colonel Sir Ben Harrison and was lord lieutenant of the county, part of his regiment in the Territorial Army had been called up and was he going to Basra in a few weeks, Bea thought Dan could give him some advice.

"Have you got any body armour?" said Dan "you want to buy yourself a yankee body Interceptor vest, it's much better than the stuff your issued with and can stop a sniper bullet. Take your issued vest and stuff it under your seat if you travel in a landy it'll save your bollocks if you meet an IED (Improvised Explosive Device)" Dan carried on while Ben listened intently "Buy yourself some really decent boots the desert wellies you get issued with are crap".

A beautiful tall leggy brunet in her mid 30s walked up behind Ben and kissed him on the cheek and said "aren't you going to introduce us darling". This was Ben's wife Lady Harrison, Dan was introduced and told her he was telling the colonel where he could get a decent drink in Basra. Dan knew from personal experience wives don't want to know when their husband's are danger. The Harrison's it turned out were Bea's neighbours they seemed to own half of North Yorkshire and were good company. Lady Harrison was upset she was sending her youngest son off to boarding school in a couple of weeks and her husband off to war.

"So how did you get the Military Cross, Major?" asked the colonel. "When I was in Afghanistan I hitched a lift across the Kandahar Province with a group of Paras to see one of my lieutenants. The convoy was hit by an RPG (Rocket Propelled Grenade) the landy I was in blew up. I got out and managed to regroup with some of the Paras, there was a bit of a fire fight and we high tailed it out of there in the last working landy" replied Dan.

Dan hated talking about active service with anyone who hasn't been there, if they've never fired a weapon in anger people just didn't understand, it was both empowering and levelling all at the same time. There was a camaraderie amongst those who had seen active service that wasn't bravado, because there was nothing that made you feel quite so scared and nothing that made you feel quite so alive. So Dan left the Lord and his Lady and wandered round the house chatting to various people, at least his shirt was a conversation starter. A night at Bea's was always different Dan chatted to the lord lieutenant and his lovely wife, a street artist who specialised in contortionism, a pig farmer and a paediatric haematologist and his very funny wife. Dan had had a good night with good company and had his fill of food and drink so went upstairs to find a bedroom.

Dan woke early and opened his bedroom door to be hit with the smell of cooking bacon. He followed his nose and went down stairs to the kitchen to find Bea, Tim and a few party goers and got stuck into some bacon sandwiches and the Sunday papers. Once he felt recovered Dan said thanks for a lovely night packed up his camp and went for a ride in the Yorkshire countryside.

Fell Walker by Peter Rankin © 2023

Chapter Twelve – An Arresting Lunch

Dan got home just after one, he showered and took his Mum for lunch. They went to Betty's a restaurant stroke café in the middle of York. Betty's was a Yorkshire institution some people came to York just to get a cup of tea and a Betty's fat rascal a big scone with loads of dried fruit. He knew it was going to be expensive but his mum really liked it so Dan thought what the hell.

Dan's mum talked she was a bit concerned about money as her tenants upstairs were moving out. She didn't like having just anyone in her flats and it took her ages to find someone suitable. She told him about her latest cause, the Mishra's a family from Tibet, they were shot at trying to leave Tibet and eventually escaped in a shipping container, they had come to the UK looking for asylum. She was still campaigning to stop the war in Iraq and her women's group that met twice a week was incensed that Iceland had decided to start whaling again.

Dan had finished off his black pudding and apple sauce it was lovely but over priced. He sat there while his mum talked at him, he loved her but once she got going she was like the Duracell bunny going on and on.

Dan had noticed that at the table next to them there was a man in his twenties by himself, he looked out of place

Fell Walker by Peter Rankin © 2023

Dan looked round he was the only lone diner in the whole restaurant. Most people who came to Betty's were either the better off local elderly or tourists, Dan thought it odd that a man in his twenties should eat alone in Betty's.

Dan's mum kept talking, she only needed the occasional nod and 'yeah' from him to reassure her that he was listening. Dan kept an eye on the next table the lad was ordering everything on the menu, what looked like a really nice lamb casserole and an expensive bottle of wine. Dan opened the menu on the table so that his mum couldn't tell he was reading it, he quickly calculated the bill for the next table it was well over £50.

Dan and his mum ordered tea just as the man on the next table ordered his coffee. Dan kept listening to his mum's words but not hearing the message. On the other side of the restaurant there was now another lad in his twenties eating by himself, when Dan looked closer he wasn't eating just having a cup of coffee.

The waitress arrived with the bill Dan got up to pay at the till "Don't forget the tip" said his mum "mother I'm nearly forty I think I know what to do in a restaurant" said Dan and shook his head. While Dan queued at the till the young man who was only drinking coffee got up and walked to the toilet, as he got next to Dan's table he stopped tied his shoe laces and then steadied himself as he stood and walked on to the toilets. "So that's your game" said Dan to himself.

Dan left the queue and went back to his table "I think we deserve a wee dram mum, lets get you a liqueur" said Dan. The waitress came over and took their drinks order just as the lad on the table next to them got up to pay his bill. "I'm just going for a jimmy riddle" said Dan and he got up and walked towards the toilets. Dan stopped in the shop area just by the entrance to the restaurant and looked at the cakes in the display cabinet. The man on the table next to Dan's had paid his bill and was walking out of the restaurant, Dan stood between him and the door and said "excuse me I think you've paid the wrong bill", the man looked panicked and quickly punched Dan in the stomach and tried to squeeze past him. But Dan had blocked the whole door space, as the man tried to slip under Dan's left arm Dan put his arms around his chest and pulled him on to the floor, then rolled on top of him and pinned the man's arms underneath himself.

The man screamed and futilely kicked at the floor, all the staff in the restaurant ran over to see what was happening. Dan pulled the man's arms up behind his back until he yelped and repositioned himself so his entire body weight was on the man's chest. The restaurant staff and customers looked on agog, all apart form Dan's mum who buried her head in her hands.

Dan found the woman who looked like she was in charge and said "I'm Detective Sergeant Cawood and this man was leaving without paying", "I've paid my fucking bill" screamed the man on the floor. "No you've paid your mate's bill" said Dan and he looked up to see an empty table on the other side of the restaurant and the emergency exit open. Never mind thought Dan half an hour in a cell and this lad will soon roll over on his best mate.

Within minutes uniform police had arrived, Dan explained that it was an old con two people go into a busy restaurant one orders everything the other just orders a drink, they swap bills the one who ordered everything just pays for a drink while the other claims to have been given the wrong bill five minutes later. Dan went back over to his mother she stared at him, he knew that stare and he knew she wasn't happy. "Sorry mum I'm gonna have to go and sort this out" said Dan.

Dan's mum left for home and he went with young lad back to the police station in the police van. While they were travelling in the van Dan studied his prey, he was about 6 inches shorter than Dan and very slim build with bleached blond hair and although he hadn't said much Dan was sure he'd heard the rounded vowels of the Lancashire mill towns. He put on a pair of latex gloves and looked through his wallet there was some money and a few cards with different names 'Mr J

Anderson' 'Darrel Peach', 'Mr Robin Small' but the driving license and two cards read 'Jason Smith'. Dan took out the driving licence and held it up to the light, to look at the holograms and photo, if it was fake it was bloody good thought Dan.

Once back at the police station Dan took Jason Smith through to the custody suite, he photocopied the contents of his wallet filled in the relevant paperwork and left him with the custody sergeant. Dan went upstairs to the incident room it was late on a Sunday afternoon and the place was dark and deserted. He put the lights on and wandered over to one of the case boards, sure enough on the one that held the details of the hotel conman, was a grainy black and white picture taken from a security camera of Jason Smith and a description of a tall very skinny man with bleached hair that Dan had remembered.

Dan checked the aliases against the names on his photocopy of Jason Smith's credit cards there were two matches. Dan got out the case folder he spent the next ten minutes flicking through the notes, there was no sign of an accomplice and the frauds were spread over the last six months. So either lunch was a one off or this pair were very careful.

Dan looked at the weekend cover list DI King was on stand by duty, he phoned him and there was no answer. Dan phoned Naz she was in the middle of unloading paving stones they had bought from B&Q and was glad of any excuse to get out of it and agreed to come in to work. Dan reckoned he had at least half an hour before Naz got in, so he changed into his spare clothes in the overnight bag under his desk. Doing an interview in shorts, sandals and an AC/DC tee shirt wouldn't look very professional.

Dan logged on to the computer and got on to the DVLA database, he pulled Jason Smith's details the license wasn't a forgery. He looked at other licenses issued to the same address and there on screen was a photo of the other man from the restaurant David Smith. They were brothers from Blackburn.

Dan checked the address in the PNC (Police National Computer). Jason and David Smith both had a number of convictions for handling stolen goods and petty theft, but nothing violent Dan noted. Dan printed everything out then went over the road to Sainsbury's and bought a packet of cigarettes.

Naz arrived in a lot less time than Dan expected. "I love driving on police business" she said as she walked in to the incident room. Dan looked at his watch whistled and said "bloody hell", "you did say it was urgent" said Naz and gave Dan her puppy dog eye stare, a look that Dan wouldn't be the first or last man to fall for.

Fell Walker by Peter Rankin © 2023

Dan briefed Naz on what happened earlier in the day and she looked over the case notes for the hotel frauds. "Look, all I want from this interview is the whereabouts of David Smith, let's leave all fraud stuff till tomorrow" said Dan. He didn't want to compromise any investigation but he didn't want let David Smith get away.

By the time Naz and Dan got into the interview room Jason Smith was waiting for them, Dan told him his rights and explained the interview procedure. Jason Smith was cock sure of himself and said he didn't need a solicitor. Dan didn't mention what had happened at Betty's but spent ten minutes going through Jason's record, as Dan talked Jason looked less and less happy. Dan took out the cigarettes and put them on table he said "here you go have one those" Jason shook as he lit the cigarette then Dan carried on "Look Jason, at the moment you and your brother have been done for a lot of property crime, but there's nothing in your record that says you're violent. Now there are some fraud charges my colleagues are going to want to talk to you about tomorrow, and we both know you're definitely going down for at least a year for them. It's up to you an easy stretch in an open prison or getting your head kicked in everyday in Cat A prison with your conviction for assaulting a police officer while resisting arrest".

Jason put his head in his hands and said "He's my fuckin' brother, I can't man". "We know who he is and we're going to arrest him sooner or later, we'd just prefer it to be sooner. So I'm prepared to forget about that thump in the stomach that lots of people saw" said Dan. There was a long silence "OK, he's in the travel lodge" said Jason with a tear in his eye. "Interview over" said Dan.

Jason Smith was escorted back to the custody suite and Naz and Dan headed off to the duty sergeants office. They explained to the sergeant what had happened and asked for some uniform back up to arrest David Smith. They then set off with two constables to the travel lodge.

Dan gave everyone a picture of David Smith taken from the NCP. When they arrived at the hotel he asked the two constables to wait in the car and keep their eyes on reception, to make sure that if the detectives missed David Smith the PC's would pick him up. There was no need for anyone to watch the back as the hotel backed on to the river Foss.

Naz and Dan asked at reception to see the duty manager, they explained to her what was happening and Dan asked if anyone was booked in under the names on Jason's credit cards. Sure enough there was a Darrel Peach in room 207. The manager gave Naz a pass key and all three of them went up to the second floor. Naz knocked at the door to room 207, David Smith answered, "Police" said Naz as she held up her warrant card. The door was slammed shut but Dan's size twelve was already in the way.

Inside the room they found David Smith and piles of various hotel linens, there were bed sheets and all sizes of towels. No wonder no-one mentioned two men in the fraud case notes the two men were almost identical thought Dan. Naz arrested David Smith and he was taken back to the police station and held in custody.

Once back at the station Dan left Naz to deal with processing David Smith and he spent the next hour typing up a report of the events of the day, but missing out a punch to the stomach. As he was typing DI King marched into the incident room and said "what the hell's goin' on, on whose authority have you been interviewing suspects?". Dan explained what had happened with the phones and the DI said he must have been in a signal black spot. For two hours thought Dan and said "was it a good film, sir", "yeah not bad" said the DI and then went bright red.

Dan explained what had happened in Betty's and how he thought he had seen a description of the Jason Smith on one of the case boards. So he had put him in custody and arrested his brother. "Good work" said the DI and Dan could tell the words stuck in the man's throat.

Fell Walker by Peter Rankin © 2023

By the time Dan got home it was getting late and he was knackered, he went upstairs to see his mum "I'm not talking to you" she said, then continued "you really showed me up today". "Would you prefer that the poor bloody waitress got the sack for giving out the wrong bills, that bloke wasn't just robbing from Betty's. Come on mum you've done enough shit jobs in your time to know what would have happened to her" said Dan. "Yeah, I suppose your right. I just don't like violence you know that" said his mum, "it was me that got hit" said Dan and shook his head. A cup of tea and a chat later they were friends again. Dan sat up with his mum smoked his pipe and watched Midsomer Murder's they both loved it, Dan for it's over the top murders with their comic overtones and his mum for John Nettles.

Dan went downstairs and crawled into his sleeping bag tired but happy, then he smiled to himself and realised with a sense of irony that he hadn't paid for his lunch at Betty's before falling into a deep sleep.

Fell Walker by Peter Rankin © 2023

Chapter Thirteen – A New Diary

Dan woke early he showered and dressed for work then headed off to McDonalds for a sausage McMuffin meal. 'I must get to the shops and buy some real food, all this junk is killing me' Dan thought to himself as he took his first bite of burger and started on The Times sodoku.

Dan walked to work he was the first person in the incident room again, he sat and flicked through the headlines before reading England's latest trouble in the test match, from the heights of the ashes victory only a year earlier it seemed no-one cared about cricket apart from Dan and a few die hard supporters.

Naz arrived at 8 and made them both a cup of tea then sat down next to Dan and said "have you been home?", "I'm just used to different hours, we always started at 07:30 in 'The Branch' and anyway I need at least an hour after waking up just to start feeling human again" replied Dan.

At spot on 8:30 DI King arrived and announced "right then everyone we've had a good result on two of our cases over the weekend, looks like I'm gonna be in the interview room all day with DC Wheeler. So you lot need to get on with some work. Hammy I want you and Jonesy working on a new case that came in over the weekend some muggings and assaults in Acomb.

Fell Walker by Peter Rankin © 2023

Wilson Marshall I want you to keep on those indecent exposures, I don't want that turning into anything worse. Bushy Danton I want you two to have a look into those burglaries that have been passed onto us by uniform." More assignments were handed out and then the DI went into his office with DC Wheeler.

Naz and Dan walked over to the board with the information about their case, it looked like there had been at least six burglaries in the past two months in the York area all with the same M.O. (modus operandi). In each case the occupants of the house were on holiday for between ten and fifteen days and when they returned home they found the place ransacked, all their valuables disappeared and their identity stolen.

Sergeant Henry Tomkins but known around the station as 'Big Harry' came into the incident room to brief Naz and Dan on the case. Judging by his accent 'Big Harry' was an Eastender, he was about the same height as Dan and a little broader around the waist. Harry had a big handlebar moustache and short white hair he was a larger than life character and a favourite of everyone in the station. "Right then lets get the important stuff out of the way, is the kettle on" said Harry.

There had been six break-ins and every scene had been attended by uniform. No prints had been found at any scene of crime. MOE (methods of entry) varied but wasn't very sophisticated, windows broken and doors jimmied open. The first two burglaries were fairly bog standard, but the last four had had documents taken and identities stolen. After the fourth break-in a pattern had been noticed and the case had been pushed up to CID.

Harry talked them through the notes from each crime. The last couple of break-ins both had a report from Jimmy Garner, he had found nothing of any worth at either crime scene but at least there were plenty of photos. Ever since CSI had appeared on TV six years earlier criminals were much more conscious about leaving bits of themselves behind at crime scenes thought Dan, but still it was his favourite TV show.

Once Harry had left Naz looked over the pile of paperwork at Dan and said "OK then where do we start?", "we need to find out what we don't know, then we can find out what we need to know" said Dan, "That's not English" replied Naz. "OK, OK, we don't know what connects each crime, so we need to find that out" said Dan "like did they cancel the milk or the papers, or did they all take the same taxi driver to the airport" said Naz. "Exactly" said Dan and thought 'at last someone trying to solve a problem'. "So who might you tell you were going on holiday?" said Naz "be careful you're starting to sound like a detective" said Dan

Naz and Dan spent half an hour thinking who might know if you were going or had gone on holiday, Naz started "the milkman, your neighbours, I always tell my hairdresser" Dan carried on "the postman, people you work with, lately the staff at McDonalds" "you eat shit, your arteries must be so furred up" said Naz.

Once they had compiled their list Naz and Dan got on the phone to all the victims of the burglaries, explained where the investigation was going and asked them a list of questions. Dan was going to write a database to cross reference the answers but just by looking both Dan and Naz could see they hadn't found a common thread to the crimes.

"Well that was a waste of a bloody morning" said Naz, "No it wasn't, just look at all the possibilities that we've eliminated" replied Dan, he paused and thought then carried on "look Naz I don't know how long you've been a DC under DI King but I don't think he's going to teach you good habits. Look at last week we shouldn't judge our job by the time it takes us to do it we're bound to miss vital things like that. We should judge it on whether we deliver justice and if the victims get some sense of closure". "I know, it's just if I wanted to push paper round a desk I'd get a job with Ian" Naz replied. Dan laughed he had two bullet scars the length of his back and an eight inch scar on his left leg that proved there was more to this than paper cuts.

It was well into the afternoon so the detectives went to canteen for a bite to eat, Naz had Italian style salad and

Fell Walker by Peter Rankin © 2023

Dan got an all day breakfast and a telling off. When they returned to the incident room they found DI King waiting for them he had a job for them that needed doing right away. They had to drive into town and find seven men willing to take part in an identity parade with Jason and David Smith. It was normally a job for uniform, but DI King wanted all hands to the pump so that the case could be handed on to the CPS before the end of the day.

Once in Town Naz approached men in their mid twenties and they thought it was their lucky day until Dan walked up with his warrant card. He was nearly laughing out loud, the shear panic on the look of the men's face was a picture. Then when Naz told them what they wanted they visibly shrunk with relief. Naz had filled the line up in less than half an hour. Dan was amazed by the power of persuasion a pretty face had, he supposed the £20 for twenty minutes work had something to do with it as well. Being in town was a mixed blessing for Dan as they walked around the foot streets they went past Scott's, a traditional pork butcher and Dan couldn't help himself he had to go in and get a pork pie. They were his absolute favourite, another mixed blessing he could no longer eat pork pies made by anyone else they just tasted bland.

Naz and Dan returned to the station in the late afternoon, they were both a bit pissed off their case wasn't going anywhere and they were doing jobs a trained monkey could have done. They spent the next hour rereading case notes and shuffling them into different orders hoping a pattern would emerge. Naz threw a stack of notes on to the table and said "I don't know. Where do we go next?", "I think we need to go back to the beginning" said Dan, Naz was listening so he carried on "if you look at the case notes in the second break-in the burglar was nearly caught by a friend feeding a cat, they didn't make that mistake again. They've only taken identity details and emptied bank accounts from the last four break-ins. Whoever is doing this is getting more and more competent so we've go to hope they made a big mistake at one of their first attempts".

Naz and Dan got on the phone to the first two victims and arranged a couple of meetings for the next day. "Well if we don't find anything tomorrow we might have to wait until these people make another mistake" said Dan. It was getting late and they were now the only people in the incident room so they called it a day and went home.

Dan walked home through the city centre, he was happy to see M&S food hall still open, he spent the next half hour picking out some really nice food and decided not to eat crap for the rest of the week.

Once into his flat he took out a blank diary and began his personal case notes for the 'fortnight holiday burglaries', within 20 minutes Dan had down all the relevant facts. When he finished Dan opened a bottle of Coniston Breweries Bluebird Bitter, he spent the next half hour making a beef stir fry and drinking beer. Dan sat and ate a huge portion of stir fry. For the first time in days he felt calm and rested so he put his feet up and fell asleep in front Television.

Chapter Fourteen – Visiting Time

Dan woke early in the chair where he had fallen asleep, he was cold, his back ached and he stank like a wino, having spilt whisky all over himself. He got up and put a few sausages in the oven then jumped in the shower, by the time he was dressed and stuck into his sausage sandwiches and mug of tea Dan was feeling decidedly better. He threw his whisky soaked clothes in the washer and looked for some clean clothes. He dressed in pair of brown cords a check shirt and blazer, in the pocket of blazer was his Old Scholar's tie he hadn't worn the jacket since his last school reunion so decided to put it on.

Dan checked his e-mails there was the usual mixed bag mostly from his friends in the forces, with photos of stunning scenery only equalled by photos of amazing carnage. There was an e-mail from the General he was at his house in Washington DC, where he acted as an advisor to the United States House Committee on Armed Services. Since the war on terror had started he found himself more and more in Washington, but he liked keeping busy and he liked keeping in touch with his Grandson. Once again the General was offering Dan tickets to the US to come and spend thanksgiving on the ranch. Dan e-mailed back to say he would go if he could get the time off work, but he would buy his own ticket.

Fell Walker by Peter Rankin © 2023

There was one more e-mail it was from his ex-wife, her solicitor had finally valued their combined estate, he got cottage in the bay and she got the flat in London, (both bought before the property market went mad). But Dan would end up paying most the majority of the debt and in return he got to keep his army pension. 'That's a bloody relief' thought Dan and for the first time he thought about his wife and their impending divorce without feeling sad. Once the legal paperwork was sorted out Dan could apply for his army pension, he had served more than 18 years and so could collect it straight away. His pension would mean that he wasn't getting deeper in debt every month and the lump sum would pay off his credit cards and leave him a bit left over.

Dan walked to work with a smile on his face, he stopped and bought the Times and also one of his little guilty secrets, a copy of Heat magazine full of celebrity pictures and gossip. Dan knew it was crap, and even took the piss out of himself for buying it, but his wife had always bought a copy and he liked to flick through the pages, and then to his own surprise started buying it for himself about two months ago.

Dan was in the incident room at just past 7am. He was the only person there, he read the Times and flicked through Heat before anyone arrived nearly an hour later. Naz turned up and made them both a cup of tea, she walked over and picked up Heat "don't tell me this is yours" she said, "'fraid so" Dan replied as his head shrunk into his neck. He was doing his little boy lost routine a common look for Dan that he was completely unaware he did.

Naz and Dan spent the next 20 minutes drinking tea and flicking through Heat like two nosey old ladies, before eventually sitting down to some work.

Naz and Dan got their case notes together before booking out a car and heading off to see the first two scenes of crime. They arrived a little early for an appointment with Shannon Davis and she invited them in for a cup of tea while she finished off her week's shopping on the internet. They had a look round the month old crime scene, Dan took photos and asked questions but nothing struck him or Naz as unusual.

A couple of hours later they found themselves at Rob Payne's House, taking similar photos and asking similar questions. Dan knew why police were called flatfoots, and he didn't think it was for walking a beat but plodding through hours of meaningless dribble before finding the one bit of evidence that made them think 'Bingo'. It was dogged persistence and the ability to read people that made Dan a good copper.

Dan was just taking photos of the garden when Naz got a call. It was Jimmy Garner he was on his way to another holiday break in, reported only ten minutes earlier. They made their excuses and left. The next break in was a few miles out of York in the village of Naburn, so Dan put on the 'blues and twos' while Naz gripped her seat and said a silent prayer.

They arrived at the scene to find Jimmy Garner in action, he had sealed off the house and they found a family sat on their garden wall with Jimmy inside taking photos. After about ten minutes Jimmy came out saying that everyone could come in. The family walked around the house and made an inventory of everything that was missing. It was usual portable electric goods, DVDs, jewellery, cash and identity.

Naz sat down with Mr Ramsay and explained what identity theft was and what it meant for him. He needed to contact anyone he had financial dealings with and cancel all credit and bank cards. He had to put a stop to all share dealings and bank accounts, account numbers needed to changed and at least for the next few weeks he needed to only use cash.

Dan went with Jimmy Garner to see the entry point, the burglars had broken a fan light window reached in and opened the kitchen window. But, Jimmy pointed out something new the broken glass had been cleared away and some plastic taped in its place. Jimmy had asked Mr Ramsay if he had cleared away the glass and he hadn't touched anything, once he knew he had been broken into he phoned the police and they asked him not to enter the house. There just where he would have expected to find broken glass Jimmy found nothing but a tiny red spot. "I think it's their first mistake, I think I've got blood and DNA, and tape is fantastic for fingerprints" said Jimmy as he pointed to the taped up window.

Dan looked round the kitchen then went outside, the back garden of the house looked over open fields and the neighbours were at least 40 yards away. The burglars could have jemmied the backdoor and no-one would have noticed. "Why the plastic?" said Jimmy as he joined Dan in the garden, "I think they've been to the house more than once, let's go and check the post" said Dan.

Dan walked through the house, unlike the other crime scenes the place hadn't been ransacked but carefully combed through. He found Mr Ramsay and asked "Was there any post when you got home?". It turned out that the normal pile of junk mail that builds up when you're away for a fortnight was not preventing the front door from opening when they first got home, there were only five letters and a free paper behind the door. "I'm really sorry Mr Ramsay I think the burglars have burgled you stole your identity and then returned a week later to pick up the credit cards they've ordered in your name. Have you and your wife checked that all your ID's are in the house Passports, Driving Licenses, birth certificates et cetera".

The Ramsays, Naz and Dan went up to the master bedroom, sure enough birth certificates and Mrs Ramsay's driving licence were missing. 'These guys are getting more sophisticated' thought Dan. They spent the next hour at the house taking statements from the Ramsays, finding photos of missing jewellery and producing a list of missing items. The Ramsays were gutted, they were nice hard working, middle class people just back from their summer holidays. Their house had been violated, their most precious possessions were missing, their credit cards had been maxed out and their savings account emptied.

Mrs Ramsay sat on the sofa staring at a photo and began to sob. Dan sat next to her to try and comfort her. She was looking at a black and white 1940s wedding photo, by the look of the woman in the picture they were her parents. "I'm very sorry" said Dan, put his arm around her checked his hanky was clean and handed it to her, "Those rings are the only things I've got left of her" sobbed Mrs Ramsay. "I know you don't think there's much chance of getting them back, but I promise I'll do everything I can to return them to you" said Dan even though he knew everything he could was very little, "Thanks" replied Mrs Ramsay and returned to searching her house.

Normally Dan met criminals in the course of his work and got to see the seedier side of life, he was used to kicking the doors into squats and meeting drug addicts who would sell their grandmother's kidney for their next hit. Even in the army he had known the dirty side of life, from war criminals in Kosovo, to 'police' in Baghdad who raped with impunity and soldiers who killed for sport. So when Dan met nice urban middle class people, with nice urban middle class lives he wondered if there was something he was missing out on. But, Dan knew if it wasn't for the thrill of the chase his job gave him, there wouldn't be much left of his life other than an army pension and the occasional night in with his mum.

Naz and Dan left for the station Jimmy was still at the house and would give them his report in the morning. Once back in the incident room they filed statements and wrote a report on the break-in. Dan contacted the fraud squad to see if he could get a lead from the identity theft, while Naz got in touch with the neighbourhood watch officer to alert them to the possible new threats the burglars posed.

The fraud squad was interested in the case and DC Khan came down to look over their case notes. He thought that the burglars were just the middlemen and were getting the information to pass on to a ring who were then using the information to max out the credit cards, "by the look of it they're new to this game but learning fast" said DC Khan "if you get a collar give me a shout I'd like to be in on any interview". By the time the DC left it was late so Naz and Dan packed up for the day and went home.

Dan walked home stopping at Marks and Spencer on the way to buy some fresh food. Once home he made a vegetable risotto and took it upstairs to his mum with a DVD. They sat and ate together watching 'four weddings and a funeral' while they drank a bottle of elderberry wine she had made last summer.

With a slightly fussy head Dan went downstairs wrote his notes for the 'fortnight holiday burglaries' case diary, crawled into his sleeping bag and fell into a deep sleep.

Fell Walker by Peter Rankin © 2023

Chapter Fifteen – Tragedy

Dan looked out of the side window of the land rover, he needed to get across the Kandahar Province to see one of his lieutenants who was supposed to be organising local police. The country was beautiful, a rocky landscape that rose into majestic mountains, scattered with brush and trees. The convoy approached a bridge, it was really a mound of dried earth covering some large drainage pipes that allowed the trickle of water to pass underneath. Every winter the almost dried out river bed would become a raging torrent as water streamed down the mountain pass, that more often than not would wash the little bridge away.

The sun streamed through the windows and warmed Dan's face he closed his eyes and was just nodding off when there was an almighty Bang, the loudest thing Dan had ever heard. He opened his eyes to find the cab of the land rover filled with smoke and blood streaming down his face. He looked around all he could see was fire and smoke, he tried to shout only to find he was completely deaf. Dan was completely disorientated he flailed out with his hands and feet while his head tried to work out which way was up. Eventually his hand caught the door handle and it swung open, by shear force of will he lunged his body out through the open door.

Fell Walker by Peter Rankin © 2023

The land rover was still on the narrow bridge and Dan came out of the door only to fall 15 feet to dried river bed below. He landed on his back and could barely breathe, he rolled onto his belly only to be sick. His whole body was a mass of pain and he had vomit in his throat, eyes and nostrils. He coughed and coughed but couldn't breathe. He pulled and pulled at the Velcro straps on his armour vest until it came free, then ripped it off. At last he sucked air into his lungs. He saw one of the drainage pipes and crawled in.

Dan sat about 15 feet inside the pipe, after a few seconds his head began to stop spinning, but pain began to shoot through his body from his back, legs and head. He shoved his left hand down the front of his trousers and into his boxers just to check everything was intact.

Dan saw a silhouette at the end of the pipe. The silhouette raised its gun. Even in this state Dan knew the profile of an AK 47. He dived forward and pulled out the browning 9mm in his belt holster. The AK 47 was firing but like most untrained gunmen he was firing too high. Dan landed fired two shots into the body mass of the silhouette and saw it drop to the ground.

Then Dan felt another shooting pain all across his back, he reached round to feel his back. His shirt was soaked with blood, obviously the silhouette hadn't shot that high.

Dan woke freezing cold and soaked with sweat, he had managed to thrash his way out of his sleeping bag. He reached round and felt the scars on his back they ran from his right shoulder right down to his backside, Dan didn't know it but touching his scars had become a nervous reaction to his recurring nightmare.

Dan dragged himself off the floor and into the shower, when he had first been blown up in the Land Rover he had spent 3 weeks in a hospital feeling sorry for himself. Now he just felt nausea and a slight out of body experience as though the whole thing had happened to someone else.

It took a real effort for Dan to get ready for work all he wanted to do was sit down and drink whisky. Dan felt sick all he could face for breakfast was a mug of tea.

He took 2 aspirins and left the flat for a long slow walk to work. The PC on the desk gave him a funny look as he entered the station, he went up to the incident room to be the first there once again. Dan looked at his watch for the first time that day, it was only 6am.

Dan sat and read through his case notes, there was something that was troubling him and he couldn't say what. He knew it wasn't the incident in Kandahar for that hadn't really left his mind since it happed, this was something else.

By the time Naz arrived at 8am Dan had begun to feel human again. They sat and looked over the case notes that Dan was now an expert on. There was nothing in the notes that was giving them an 'in' to this case. All the properties were broken into without a seemingly common thread.

At 9:30 Jimmy Garner turned up he had his crime scene report, the photos were just how Dan remembered seeing the scene. He had sent the blood sample off to the DNA lab and now all they could do was wait and hope there was a match with the home office database.

Naz and Dan went down to the canteen for a break, half way through his cup of tea Dan got a call on his mobile phone. He didn't recognise the number but knew it was a Whitby number, just a couple of miles up the coast from Robin Hood's Bay. Dan hated mobile phones but knew he had to have one for work, so he just let the phone ring on the table. Naz looked at Dan impatiently "can you turn that bloody thing off? it's embarrassing, everyone is looking at us" said Naz and answered the phone for him. Everyone was two uniform PCs and a catering assistant cleaning up. Naz had an irrational fear of anyone hearing her mobile phone ring and was acutely embarrassed when either her own or Dan's phone rang. Dan secretly thought it was very funny and had downloaded the 'crazy frog' ring tone and had turned the volume up as loud as he could.

"This is the phone of DS Cawood can I help you" said Naz in her very posh phone voice. After a brief conversation Naz gave Dan the phone and said "I think you'd better take this". It was the Whitby police a body had been found at the bottom of the cliffs halfway between Whitby and Robin Hood's Bay. There was no identification on the body but in the pocket of the jeans was £500 and piece of paper with Dan's mobile number on it. "Oh fuck" said Dan, dropped the phone and buried his head in his hands.

Naz picked up the phone and Dan said a prayer silently hoping the body was someone else's. Naz was explaining what was happening and Dan signalled her to give him the phone. "Is this body about 6'4", athletically thin with long unkempt hair and in his mid-twenties" said Dan and went white when he got the reply then carried on "His name's Josh and I think his surname is Filmore, I'm sorry about this but his but he's a US citizen and his father works at the embassy in London".

Dan spent the next fifteen minutes explaining how he had met Josh and how Josh had ended up with his number. Josh's body had been found at the bottom of 200 feet high cliffs by an early morning dog walker on the coastal footpath, anything he was carrying and one of his shoes had been washed out to sea the only thing that could identify him was Dan's number. Dan agreed to go to Whitby and identify the body and give a statement.

Dan finished his tea and went to see DI King, he would need the rest of the day off, and the little voice at the back of his head that had whispered there was something wrong with John Carter's murder was now screaming and shouting. "We need to investigate the death of this American lad, he is a potential witness to a murder" said Dan to DI King, "Oh I think from what you've said this accident was just a coincidence" replied DI King before dismissing Dan. Dan would record this meeting in his own notes, he had always found that in murder cases there was no such thing as coincidental accidents.

Dan got a lift home from uniform put on his biking leathers and rode over to Whitby. He loved the ride from York to Whitby there was a stretch of dual-carriageway that let Dan open up the Triumph Triple way beyond the legal limit but he thought 'what the hell I'm on Police business'. After that the road turned into a narrow winding country lane that climbed onto the North Yorkshire Moors. Dan rode through the desolate but beautiful landscape, this was his place and all he felt was the motorbike beneath him and all he could think about was the view. For the first time in a long time Dan's mind was blank and he was happy.

Dan arrived at Whitby Police Station showed his warrant card and was ushered to comfy side room and given a cup of tea. He guessed that if he wasn't a copper this meeting would be more of an interview in a lot less comfy surroundings.

After about 20 minutes a uniform sergeant took Dan on the five minute walk to Whitby Community Hospital. There Dan was able to identify the disfigured body of Josh Filmore, Dan had seen a lot of corpses over the course of his career, but the death of someone young and full of life made him realise how fragile he really was. Dan felt a sadness he hadn't expected, he'd only known this amiable rogue for about week and yet he felt a weariness in his heart. Dan said a silent prayer and was escorted back to the police station.

DI Richard Green came into the room and introduced himself, he chatted to Dan for the next hour. DI Green told Dan how and when the body had been found. Josh was at the base of a cliff just south of Saltwick Beach, he had been repeatedly tossed against the rocks by waves that had ripped his clothes and caused multiple post mortem cuts and abrasions. From the Police doctor's preliminary findings they knew that Josh had multiple broken bones and crush injuries typical of a very high fall.

Dan told the DI how he had met Josh three weeks earlier while doing the coast to coast walk, how they had walked together and how Josh ended up staying at his cottage in Robin Hood's Bay. Dan also told the DI the story of the murder of John Carter and how Josh was a potential witness.

"Who's running the Carter murder?" asked DI Green, "DI King has handed the case over to the CPS" replied Dan. "Oh! Bloody hell who gave that prat a murder, I wouldn't trust him with a rubber wheelbarrow" said DI Green. DI Green had worked with DI King and didn't like him as a person or trust his judgement as a police officer, Dan was warming to DI Green. "Look sir, I don't think the Carter murder should have been signed off without some further investigation. I just feel that there's more to it than meets the eye and I can't believe the accidental death of a witness is just a coincidence. Your sergeant said he had £500 in his pocket, and I know for a fact he didn't have a pot piss in so where did the money come from?" said Dan. "Well Sergeant how can I help you?" asked the DI, "Bea Gerry the local Home Office Pathologist is a friend of mine, could you have the body sent to her and tell her I think there's something a bit fishy, she likes a challenge". DI Green agreed to treat Josh Filmore's death as suspicious and would contact Bea as soon as possible.

Fell Walker by Peter Rankin © 2023

Dan walked into the town centre and bought a few essentials milk, a loaf of bread and a bottle of Islay single malt. Then he went over to the harbour and down the little cobble streets in the old town that Captain Cook would have walked down before leaving for his voyage of discovery. Today though rather than ropes and chandlery they were selling souvenirs and cream teas. Right at the end of the row of houses down by the sea was Fortune's Kippers, a traditional smokehouse that produced the best kippers in the world. The only thing that had changed here in the last hundred years was yesterday's newspapers that Dan's pair of kippers were wrapped in.

Dan wandered back to his motorbike outside the police station and rode the 6 miles down the road to his little cottage in Robin Hood's Bay. Once inside Dan sat down took out the John Carter case diary from his bag and wrote down the events of the day.

Next he phoned Naz and asked for a favour "listen tomorrow I need some cover, I want you to log down that we are seeing one of the past crime scenes. You can go by yourself if you want to or you can meet me at the hospital to see an autopsy" he said. Naz agreed with some glee she had never seen full autopsy and liked the idea of a little bit of conspiracy.

Dan's second call was to an old friend for another favour. "Bea, I've got a funny feeling about this one, please pull rank and make sure you get the case and please can I be there. I think there's a woman in prison who shouldn't be there" he said. Bea agreed she liked a puzzle and she liked Dan, the two together she couldn't resist. DI Green had already been in touch and Bea was having the body sent to York, she would do the preliminary work tonight and the autopsy tomorrow at 6am sharp.

Dan phoned Naz again and told her where and when the autopsy would be. Then he went out to the Dolphin Inn where he consoled the landlady over the recent death of one of her dogs and tucked into a succulent rare ribeye steak, his favourite. Dan returned to the cottage, with his nightmare still fresh in his mind he didn't to go to bed, but he set his alarm and fell asleep in the arm chair cradling a glass of whiskey.

Chapter Sixteen – Secret Meeting

Dan's alarm got him up at 4am, he showered and put on some clean clothes he found in the drawers upstairs. The trousers were a very snug fit and Dan knew he needed to eat less and do more. He sat down to grilled Fortune's kippers and toast for breakfast, a rare treat. Then set off on the triumph across Fylingdale moor with the sun rising over the sea in the background, a sight that Dan would never cease to find beautiful.

Dan was the only thing on the road over the top of the deserted moor, so he put the hammer down and tested his nerve to the limit arriving outside York District Hospital just after 5:30am. There waiting in her car in the Car Park was Naz. She got out of the car ran over to Dan excited and bright eyed "I haven't slept all night, I'm so excited, can we go in now" said Naz. She was like a giddy little schoolgirl, Dan couldn't remember his first autopsy but he was sure he wasn't this excited, in fact he remembered a feeling of dread.

Naz and Dan went into the hospital. Dan was knackered he had had 5 hours sleep in the last two days and identified the body of someone who he liked, whilst Naz acted like a spinning top on speed. They arrived at Bea's office and were invited in for a cup of tea.

Fell Walker by Peter Rankin © 2023

With the niceties of life over and introductions made Bea got down to business. First she explained that time of death was difficult to estimate as the body had landed on rock then sometime later been cooled by sea water so core body temperature couldn't be used and they would be better off using tide tables. Then she went over the multiple Post Mortem abrasions and breaks she had found on the corpse, showing them photos and X-rays. She concluded that they must have been caused by the tide battering the body against the cliffs. Then Bea showed a new set of photos and X-rays the so-far only anti-mortem injury she could find a broken neck, smashed skull and crushed vertebrae caused by blunt force trauma, almost certainly the result of the fall.

"How do you know if a wound is Post-Mortem?" asked Naz, "if the heart isn't beating then there is no blood pressure, so when a blood vessel is damaged one doesn't see the same bruising pattern or get any spurting blood from arteries that have been cut open" replied Bea while Dan studied the photographs and X-rays. "Right then, on to the butchers block" said Bea.

Dan dressed in his 'greens' quickly so that by the time Bea and Naz got in the room he was moving the spot light over Josh's washed, athletic and broken body examining it inch by inch. Bea just stood back and let Dan get on with it whilst Naz moved very slowly toward the corpse, as she got closer the look of excitement was being replaced with the look of dread, Dan was secretly pleased.

Dan moved from the feet to the head, when he got to the neck he looked over at Bea and said "Can you come and move the head for me please". Bea walked over and lifted the head Dan took out a torch and looked at the back of the neck "can we turn the corpse over please" Dan added, so the three of them carefully on Bea's instruction turned the body over.

Dan left the autopsy room and returned moments later with the photos from Bea's desk, he rifled through them until he found photos of the neck. "There!" he said and pointed to three marks on the neck that weren't on the photo, just under the left ear were three barely visible round bruises in a line. "What is it?" said Naz, Dan reached his hand toward the corpse and asked Bea "may I?" "Of course dear boy" was the reply.

Dan spread out the first three fingers on his right hand and moved them towards the bruises hovering over the skin but not touching the body. "There" he said and then walked over to Naz. He stood in front of her, gently put her hands around his neck, and said "squeeze tight and look where your fingertips end up". Naz squeezed gently and sure enough the first three fingers on her right hand ended up spread out in a line just below Dan's left ear.

Bea moved over to the body and took multiple photos of the neck, "Why weren't bruises there yesterday?" asked Naz. "The sea water must have acted as an ice pack and reduced the swelling, and so the bruises took some time to develop post-mortem" replied Bea.

Bea ushered everyone back to her office and explained that due to the changing nature of this case, now that bruises had been found on the neck she really needed to get in touch with DI Green, because he could no longer treat this as accidental death. Sneaking someone in to view the post-mortem of an accidental death was bending the rules, but sneaking someone in to the post-mortem of a murder victim could jeopardise any future prosecution.

Naz and Dan drove back to his flat just down the road to regroup. Dan was relieved he didn't want to see Josh cut open, while Naz was relieved and disappointed all at the same time. The total lack of life in the corpse had been a real shock to her, but once there she had wanted to see an autopsy just to get it over with. The fast talking and hyperactivity were just Naz's way of being nervous.

Dan made them both a cup of tea and they decided to keep the events of today to themselves, as pretty soon

John Carter's murder would be back open. Dan got changed into a shirt and trousers as they talked. "Shit! What happened to your back" said Naz as she stared at the two parallel scars that ran the full length of his back and into the waistband of his trousers. "They're my lucky stripes" said Dan, "Why unlucky?" asked Naz. "If the bullets had been two inches lower that would have been unlucky" replied Dan.

"The DCI (detective chief inspector) will be back on Monday, you'll be able to explain everything then" said Naz, "well I hope he listens better than DI King" replied Dan. "you'll like him" said Naz, "what's he like" said Dan "Have you met Bella Stella" said Naz and Dan replied with a grin on his face "yes I have had the privilege of meeting Chief Superintendent Davis". "DCI Shaw and CS Davis couldn't be more different. She's all forms, courses and reports, he wants results but he's an old fashion copper, I wouldn't be surprised if he had a bottle of whisky in his desk" said Naz. 'Good' thought Dan the last thing he needed was a boss who wanted forms filling, new initiatives started and ridicules targets to meet. Dan had been lucky in his army career, despite working for the government when you're in a war zone no one gives a toss about targets, forms and political correctness just results.

"One thing that needs explaining is that £500" said Dan thinking out loud, then carried on "Josh didn't

Fell Walker by Peter Rankin © 2023

have a bean, I walked with him for over a week and he was going without food to buy cigarettes. I let him have some money I had ferreted away at the cottage but, there was no more than £50". Naz interrupted Dan's thought process "can we get serial numbers from the notes, we should be able to trace them back to the region they were issued in at least". "Good I like that" said Dan, he would give DI Green a ring and find out.

Naz and Dan returned to the station to try and make some head way the case they were supposed to be working on. Neither of them had there hearts in it, Dan phoned DI Green and he was already seeing if he could track down the movements of the bank notes through the Bank of England and the major clearing banks. DI Green promised to phone Dan as soon as he had the results.

Naz and Dan arranged to go out and look at one of their crime scenes not because they thought it would help their case, but once out of the incident room they were free to talk about the events of this morning. Naz was really excited and couldn't stop talking about it.

In just over a week she and Dan had forged a good working relationship, and Dan hoped the start of a friendship. It was unusual for Dan to be working with someone again, ever since he had been promoted captain nearly 15 years earlier he had been in command. There had been lots of people who had worked for him, some he thought of as friends, but Dan had always thought he liked working alone.

They arrived at the scene of the third burglary, this was the first that Jimmy Garner had attended and Dan had read the detailed crime scene report over and over in the last couple of days. Dan spent 5 minutes walking around the outside of the house 'they're learning' he thought, the first couple of break-ins had been in crowded estates, this one was on the edge of the pretty village of Bishopthorpe with the gardens looking over open fields and the river beyond. The burglars were getting better all the time, avoiding crowded estates, keeping away from pets and stealing identities.

Dan and Naz walked down the garden path and knocked at the door. They were shown the crime scene, just like the photos Dan had seen only tidy. They were given tea and biscuits and listened to the tale of Mrs Johnson's missing cat that lived next door.

After battling their way through rush hour traffic Naz and Dan returned to the station to find the incident room emptying as everyone went home. It had been an empty kind of day altogether for Dan, the fact that he been proved right that there was more to John Carter's death was a hollow victory, especially when it cost the life of his friend. His own case was going nowhere and Dan was frightened of going to sleep because the nightmares had started again. Just as he was starting to feel sorry for himself he realised there was one ray of light that had come out of today, he was working with someone he liked and trusted.

"Come on Sir, I'll get you a pint on your way home" said Naz, so they both set off for the local and a quick drink before home. Dan eventually arrived home weary but feeling happier than when he woke up. He went upstairs and sat and chatted to his mum. She recognised the signs, whenever he returned from a particularly tough overseas posting he would take a few days leave and just sit and chat. They didn't talk about anything serious but managed to talk into the early hours and put a dent in a bottle of single malt, his mum even let Dan smoke his pipe in the living room. Dan fell asleep on the sofa so his mum put a blanket over him kissed him on the forehead and turned out the light.

Chapter Seventeen – Just Walking the Dog

Dan woke at 4am he had had a fitful night's sleep and it was still dark outside. He went down stairs and spent the next half hour in the shower trying to wash away the shadow of death, but he knew it wouldn't work. He had spent all his working life around death and normally Dan could detach himself from it by mentally putting it in a box never to be opened again. But, when it got personal he wasn't immune to normal feelings and the sense of uselessness that surrounded death, knowing that whatever you do you can't fix the situation had been with him since he had heard about Josh's death.

Dan was starving and there was nothing in the fridge so he headed upstairs to see if there was anything edible in his mother's kitchen. Once through the door he found Frisky running round his ankles looking for attention. He stood in the kitchen trying to keep Frisky quiet by stroking her with his foot and rifling through the lentils and chickpeas looking for something to eat. There at the back of the freezer was an out of date packet of Linda McCartney vegetarian sausages, so Dan made himself sausage sandwiches for breakfast and shared them with Frisky.

At first light Dan took Frisky out for a walk, they wandered down to the river and out on to the Ings half an hour's walk away. They got to the spot where just over a week ago Dan had stopped and chatted to a group of teenagers camping. There on the river bank were the burnt out remains of a tent surrounded by empty charred beer cans.

At first Dan stood and stared at the mess on the riverbank shaking his head, then he noticed about 100 yards further up the bank Frisky sniffing round a burnt out mini-motorbike. It must have been the same one that woke up the campers a week ago.

A thought suddenly occurred to Dan it was what had been bugging him for the last few days. He needed to check some notes to answer the questions that were running round in his head. He shouted across the ings "come on Frisky you clever little thing, we've got a case to solve". Dan started walking quickly towards home, then picked Frisky up and broke into a run the questions in his head were getting louder and louder.

Once home Dan was sweating and breathing heavily, he was out of shape and knew he needed to do something about it. Once he had his breath back he opened up the case diary for John Carter's Murder. Dan didn't have the official statements but he had a copy of all the statements people had wrote in the pub while waiting for the police. Dan searched through them and pulled out all the ones from the campers who had slept outside in the field next to the car park.

Fell Walker by Peter Rankin © 2023

All the school pupils had written down the same, made tea, washed up and in bed for an early night. The other couple camping outside had quite a different story to tell. In the pub drinking then kept awake by the noisy school children until 4:30am, then rudely awakened at 6am by some crashing and banging. Dan had talked to Josh that morning and he knew he had been kept awake most of the night, but his statement said early night followed by a good night's sleep. But, no one who slept outside mentioned hearing a car. No car no Mrs. Carter thought Dan.

So whoever the murderer was, was either in the pub already or arrived on foot between 4:30 and 6am. The crash and bang at the back of the pub at 6am could have been someone climbing in, because the first people to wake up were the staff at 6:30.

Dan put on his work clothes and walked quickly into work arriving in the incident room at 7am. He had his case diary from John Carter's murder and sat and read through it till more people arrived nearly an hour later. Eventually DI King arrived at 8:30 and Dan followed him into his office.

"Well Danton what can you do for me?" said the DI. "I think you need to reopen the Carter case, Sir" replied Dan and then while DI King was still taken aback carried on "The corpse I identified two days ago was a potential witness to the Carter murder, when his body was found there was £500 in his pockets and yet I know for a fact he was penniless. I have spoken to DI Green in Whitby and they suspect foul play, I think you're looking at a double murder Sir". DI King was thinking as Dan spoke and then said "so you think Mrs Carter had an accomplice", "No Sir, I think Mrs Carter is innocent. If you go through the witness statements no-one was woken by a car through the night, yet lots of other noise kept them a wake" said Dan.

There were no official statements from any of the school children at the Lion Inn on the night of the murder and Dan knew the unofficial statements didn't tell the truth. They needed to know if the pupils had seen anything whilst running round all night, because without knowing it they might have seen the murderer. DI King didn't want to reopen the case, today was his last day in charge of CID before the DCI came back from his holidays' on Monday. But, he would prefer to do this, rather than let the DCI reopen the case for him next week. "OK Danton I'm not going to put a stop to Mrs Carter's prosecution till we know more. I'm going to contact DI Green and I want you to get those statements" said the DI and with that Dan was dismissed.

Dan walked over to Naz and asked her for a favour and then scrounged a lift home from uniform. Naz phoned Keswick community college and Tertiary education centre. She needed to get their permission for Dan to conduct interviews and take statements from everyone who camped outside the Lion Inn the night of John Carter's murder. Once she had the school's agreement she needed them to provide Dan with a room and an adult to sit in on the interview, the headmaster agreed to do that. Then she had to phone round the parents of the children and get their permission for the interviews.

While Naz spent the morning on the phone Dan raced across the Yorkshire Dales and over the Lakeland fells to Keswick community college and Tertiary education centre. Once there Dan took off his biker's leathers and tried to look professional and went into the school.

Dan had a few minutes with the headmaster before interviewing the pupils, he agreed that the pupils could be completely candid in their statements and they wouldn't get into trouble at school as there was a greater truth that needed to be discovered. Dan conducted seven interviews and wrote down seven statements, one of the boys from the trip was off school ill. Dan could only remember Suzie from the Lion Inn, she was the pretty, forthright young lady and seemed pleased to have been remembered giving the others a smile that said 'I told you so'.

All the statements said the same thing, the pupils had waited till the light went out in John Carter's room, they knew which one was his because he had waved at them as they put their tents up. Then at about 11pm they shared the bottle of Bacardi that James had brought and smoked the cigarettes that Suzie had brought, whilst playing games in the field like stuck in the mud and hide and seek. Once they were all a little drunk they played strip poker and ran around the campsite in their undies. An American had told them all to 'shut the fuck up' several times during the night and they eventually went to bed at around 5:00am when the American told a naked James he would break his legs if he tripped over his guy ropes again (and they all believed he meant it). As they told their tale of drunken debauchery Dan felt most sorry for the Headmaster, he was obviously embarrassed and he guessed things would be tightened up in future.

Three of the pupils heard an almighty bang at around 6am but the rest slept through it. Suzie was the only one to investigate it, she looked out of her tent and didn't see anything, but heard more crashing and banging from the big shed at the back of the pub. One of the other girls had crawled into the boys' tent and her and her boyfriend spent the whole night 'cuddling but nothing more honest', they didn't get any sleep until the minibus ride home with the headmaster. But, the most important thing from Dan's point of view no-one heard a car until well after breakfast.

Fell Walker by Peter Rankin © 2023

Dan had the statements signed and witnessed, thanked the Headmaster for his hospitality then set off for York as fast as he could. Once the school was out of sight he stopped and phoned DI King to give him the news. The DI thanked Dan and said he would 'take it under advisement'. By the time Dan got back to York it was nearly 8pm and the weekend had begun, so he headed straight home.

Dan spent the night with a take out from the curry house and 6 bottles of Black Sheep Bitter because they were on special at Sainsbury's local. Then settled down to a Coen Brothers film marathon eventually falling asleep having watched 'Oh Brother Where art Thou', 'The Big Lebowski' and 'Miller's Crossing'.

Fell Walker by Peter Rankin © 2023

Chapter Eighteen – Labour Day

Dan had only been asleep for 3 hours when his phone woke him at 8am. It was Naz "yeah what do you want" he said as he tried to work out who he was, "I've got a case for us to get through" replied Naz. It turned out that the case in question was a case of beer and in return for a bed, beer and as much vegetarian chilli as Dan could eat, Naz was offering a days labouring on their barn conversion.

Dan dressed in his shorts and an old U.S. marines' t-shirt he'd swapped for a para's beret during the first Gulf War, he packed his rucksack and set off for Naz's. He stopped at McDonalds and bought two sausage McMuffins as it would be the only meat Dan ate for the next 24 hours. Then he took the Harrogate bus and got off at the stop nearest Naz's house and walked the last couple of miles to the barn.

The approach to the barn was down a farm track and from a distance it looked beautiful, a perfect dales barn in an ideal country setting. As Dan got closer the setting didn't change but the barn looked like it had been bombed and Dan had seen enough bombed buildings in his time to know. The roof was shot and part of one wall had collapsed, the track Dan was walking down wouldn't be useable in winter and he could see no signs of mains services.

Round the back of the barn were a couple of dilapidated concrete prefab outbuildings and a static caravan in nearly as bad a state as the barn and between them were a pile of building materials and Ian and Naz trying to move them. Even dressed in work clothes and boots Naz looked gorgeous, but Dan could tell neither her or Ian had a clue what they were doing.

Once at the barn Dan was put to work, he helped Ian shift a few tons of paving stones, demolished an old out house and put the pieces in the skip. Just like most men Dan loved demolition, building was fine, decorating was a pain in the arse and soft furnishings were like being slowly tortured to Dan. But, demolition that was the thing he swung the sledge hammer with glee, so that all the injuries and wounds from nearly twenty years in the army were hurting like a bastard. Dan just gritted his teeth and smashed through the concrete, he loved it.

Dan and Ian worked until last light, Naz had spent most of the afternoon instructing Ian where to put the York stone slabs on the drive so they looked right then spent the evening in the Kitchen. With work over the three of them sat down to a hearty supper and the case of Stella that had spent the afternoon in an old tin bath full of ice.

They talked about the barn, Ian showed Dan where they were going to have to underpin the gable end of the barn as there were no foundations and how he would have to dig a huge hole in the garden to put in a septic tank. Naz talked of the wooden staircase she wanted making and putting through the centre of the building. She showed Dan bathroom catalogues and paint swatches. By the time they had finished Dan was certain it would be a lovely home in a few years time but one that he couldn't afford.

Naz and Ian had bought the barn at a property auction they had gone to, to buy a disused pub in Knaresborough but the price had risen too high and bought the barn with planning permission without seeing it instead. Naz fell in love with it at the auction, but it cost every penny they could raise between them so they had been working on it themselves for the last four months.

Dan couldn't quite work out where four months work had gone, but they had bought the caravan and had to provide all their own services. They had a generator for electricity, gas bottles for heating and cooking and a stand pipe for water, but no mains sewage. Naz moaned that she hadn't had a hot bath for four months and Ian promised to get a water heater rigged up before winter.

After supper and the tour through the grand plan talk inevitably turned to murder. Dan was still worried that Judith Carter wasn't the murderer and felt certain that

Fell Walker by Peter Rankin © 2023

Josh Filmore's death wasn't a coincidence. Talking about legal matters Ian was on much firmer ground than DIY and Dan was happy to see that he had a good no nonsense grasp of the law. Ian listened to Dan and Naz talk, then he analysed the case. He could see the case against Judith Carter but would like the chance to defend her. Then Ian told both Naz and Dan off for getting involved with the Josh Filmore case and finished with, "if for nothing else, if you get in to trouble who is going to knock down our other concrete bunkers".

As they got more drunk the three of them talked and put the world to rights, once he had enough beer in him Dan began with his dirty jokes. Ian and Naz wanted to know about Dan's career in the army, Naz knew about his military cross and wanted to know how he got it. As usual Dan played down his medals and made his eighteen years in the army sound like one desk job after another. "yeah right" said Naz "so what are those scars down your back?" Dan smiled and with that the night was brought to an end. It was a beautiful summer's night Ian turned off the generator and the site was shrouded in darkness. Dan loved the sky at night he crawled under a blanket out in the open and fell asleep, trying to remember the names of the constellations.

Fell Walker by Peter Rankin © 2023

Chapter Nineteen – Easy Rider

Dan woke at 6am the birds were singing and the sky was already blue, he loved sleeping in the open. His head was a little befuggled from last nights excess and his body sore from yesterday's exertions but Dan felt great. He got up and walked over the nearby fields sucking fresh air into his lungs glad to be alive.

Dan walked for nearly two hours before returning to the barn, he sat down with Naz and Ian to a breakfast of porridge and fruit juice and thought that it was nice for a change but not for everyday. They talked some more and Dan left for home at 9am. He walked to the main road and took the bus home.

Dan got home with an arm full of Sunday papers and went upstairs to see his mum. They sat for an hour drinking tea and reading funny stories from the papers to each other, eventually Dan said "come on let's get on the bike and go in to the country for Sunday dinner". There was a pub on the moors that Dan was drawn to and any excuse he could use to get out there he would right now.

Dan had a shower and got dressed in his leathers and lent his mum an old jacket she could use on the bike. His mum had bought him an intercom for his helmets last year for Christmas and Dan knew the price of visiting the Lion Inn was his mother asking if they were going too fast at least twenty times. They eventually set off on the bike, Dan's mum clung on to him for dear life and complained about the speed, while Dan travelled at the most pedestrian of paces hoping no-one would see them.

It was late summer and a beautiful summer's afternoon Dan took the back roads all the way if he was going to have to go slow he was going to enjoy the view. There were cars and families everywhere trying to enjoy the last few days of summer. By the time they got to the Lion Inn Dan felt like the blood had been cut of from his legs his mum was clung on so tight.

The car park was full and when they went into the bar the place was packed they just got their order in for food before the kitchens closed for the afternoon. There was no sign of the landlord or landlady but the two Polish girls were running themselves ragged serving food and clearing tables. Once they had a table to sit at Dan said "I just want to go and check on the bike, I can't remember if I locked the steering".

Dan shot out of the pub and walked quickly round the back of the building, he stood where Josh had pitched his tent two weeks earlier and looked at pub. From the front the pub was a chocolate box cottage, but it was from the back you really got a feeling for how the building had organically grown over two hundred years. Dan looked at the out buildings leaning up

Fell Walker by Peter Rankin © 2023

against the back wall of the pub and tried to remember what Josh had said to him over breakfast 'Man last night was fucked up, the guy in that blue tent snored like a pig, those high school kids they were in and out of each others tents till 4:30am, then someone started kicking ass in those sheds over there and then a bloody sheep woke me at 6am'. Dan wandered over to what he presumed Josh meant by the sheds, but they were all locked up. Through the gaps in the doors he could just see what looked like and smelt like rubbish.

Dan ran back into the pub, after Betty's last weekend if his mum knew he had come out here because of work his life wouldn't be worth living. As if to tempt fate as soon as he sat down his mum asked "so how did you find this place?", "I stayed here when I did the coast to coast" said Dan not wanting to lie to his mum.

Dan and his mum sat for age waiting for their food as the place was so busy, but they didn't really care as they sat and chatted. They talked about Dan's divorce and what he was going to do now he had access to his army pension. Dan wanted to get a place of his own but he didn't want to leave his mum in the lerch so he wouldn't move out until she had found another new tenant.

His mum's tenants were never just paying customers they always came with a bad luck story and occasionally left leaving unpaid bills. But for the most part she helped people out when they were at their lowest and when times came good they would find a way to repay her. Every Wednesday evening a Chinese meal would be delivered to the house with a bottle of wine it was from her first tenant Mr Wong. He had arrived in England with nothing from China nearly thirty years ago and with Dan's mum's help he had brought his family over from China and set up his own take away business that was now a thriving restaurant run by his son. Dan's mum was well loved and he knew she had far more friends than he would ever have.

Their meals arrived and Dan was told off again for his carnivorous ways as tucked into a lovely steak and kidney pudding, while his mum had the vegetarian stroganoff. While they were eating one of the waitresses came over with another meal and said "do you mind if I sit here sergeant? the rest is busy and I have finished work".

Dan looked at the lovely Janna and her beautiful eyes and said "of course", then he looked over at his mum and she gave him a very hard stare and mouthed the word 'Sergeant'. Dan knew he was in the shit when he got home.

The three of them ate their meal and chatted Dan's mum asked "so how did you meet the sergeant?" and as Janna told the story of a murder Dan shrank into his chair. Eventually the conversation turned to less

Fell Walker by Peter Rankin © 2023

morbid matters, Dan listened as Janna and his mum talked of Poland and family back home. He found himself staring and was quite content to be sat with these two ladies just drifting along on their conversation while he smoked his pipe.

They sat in the bar till early evening then set off home for York, as soon as they were on the bike with the intercom connected Dan's mum began telling him off for taking her to a crime scene, it didn't stop until they got home. Once home Dan was desperate for a pint he had spent all day watching other people drink while he sipped at his tea. So he wandered down to his local and propped the bar up by himself to drink a belly full of beer. Dan left the pub tired and merry he walked down to the river and skimmed stones across the surface of the water before making his way home to bed.

Fell Walker by Peter Rankin © 2023

Chapter Twenty – A Working Lunch

Dan woke early out of habit but felt rough as a dog and spent half an hour in the shower trying to wash the groggy feeling out of his hair. He dressed and walked to work, on his way through town he grabbed a bacon sandwich and a take out tea from the local bakery.

Dan arrived to find the incident room empty, he really didn't feel like work and sat down to read the Times. By the time Naz arrived at 8am he had read the headlines, completed the Soduku and given up on the crossword. They sat and drank tea and Naz told Dan how Ian and her had finished laying the patio on Sunday and how the whole thing was coming along.

As they were drinking their tea a call came in, there had been another burglary. It was another house over looking fields with everything including identities stolen. Dan got in touch with Jimmy Garner to meet them at the house, while Naz went to find DC Khan in the fraud squad office. By 9am the three of them were on their way to Knapton an urbanised village on the Northern edge of York. While they were in the car Dan asked DC Khan for a favour "any chance you could trace the source of these bank notes?" and handed over a list of the serial numbers of the notes found on Josh Filmore and with his agreement DC Khan was brought into the conspiracy.

Fell Walker by Peter Rankin © 2023

They arrived at the house to find a sun tanned family mother, father and two young daughters standing in the drive shivering in their holiday clothes. Dan got out of the car showed his warrant card and introduced everyone. Mr and Mrs Maguire had just got back from their condo in Florida and discovered their house broken into and empty. They had reported the crime and been advised not to go into the house until the police arrived. Unfortunately Dan didn't want them to go into the house until the scene of crimes officer arrived.

Once Jimmy Garner arrived he and Dan put on scene suits and wandered round the house. There were no electric or white goods left in the house and every drawer and cupboard was ransacked and emptied on the floor. The whole house stank of rotting food as the burglars had emptied the American style fridge freezer on the kitchen floor before stealing it. Once in the kitchen they found the pile of rotting food wriggling with maggots it had been sat in the sunlight under the kitchen window for at least a week by the look of it, the kitchen window had been smashed. But, once again the culprits had left nothing but an empty house and broken lives.

Once Jimmy had documented the scene and was happy he couldn't he couldn't get any more evidence Dan went outside to speak to Mr Maguire. "Has your wife been in the house yet?" Dan enquired, "No, why?" replied Mr Maguire, "well the house is in a state and if your wife and daughters go in they will be really upset, can I suggest that DC Bush drives them to a friends house or a hotel while we sort things out in there". With that Naz took a protesting Mrs Maguire and her daughters to a hotel while Dan DC, Khan and Mr Maguire cleaned up the mess in the kitchen.

The burglars had stepped up their game again Dan thought white goods and furniture this time, leaving behind a wreck of a house. Once the kitchen was clean and the wind started to blow the smell out of the house Dan and Mr Maguire wandered around and tried to work out what was missing. While DC Khan tried to workout what paperwork and ID were missing from the house, he advised Mr Maguire what to do with his personal finances and gave him leaflets on how to deal with Identity theft. Then he wrote down what credit cards he currently held in his name, he would cross reference this with the credit reference agencies when he got back to the station to see if there were any other cards in his name or any strange activities on his accounts.

Dan felt desperately sorry for the Maguire's they were just normal people, who five hours ago would have felt great having just come back from a relaxing family holiday. Now their life was in shattered and their home in bits.

Once Naz had returned with the car they all returned to the police station. As they walked through the car park of the station one of the uniform WPCs ran up to Naz conspiratorially and whispered something to her. "What was that?" asked Dan not wanting to miss out on the gossip. "The DCI's back from holiday and he's not happy, he spent the morning with DI King sorting out the murder case. I think you're in the sticky brown stuff" said Naz. "Oh! Bloody hell I haven't even met the man yet" said Dan as he shook his head.

Naz and Dan returned to the incident room it was late in the afternoon, Dan had just sat down when his phone rang he answered and heard "Good afternoon Sergeant, look your left" Dan turned his head there was a jovial man sat in the DCI's office with the door propped open waving at him. "Mine's white with two sugars, make us both a cuppa then pop in for a chat".

Dan made the teas and popped in the office for a chat "So you're our man from the Met" said the DCI, "not exactly what I'd call a good start Cawood, I've come back from holiday relaxed and de-stressed to find I'm in the middle of a right royal, ocean going fur lined fuck up". The DCI was of average height and carried the belly of someone who liked their beer, Dan had been warned he was a happy go lucky character when everything was going well but a bugger when it wasn't. The DCI spoke with an accent from the Yorkshire dales and had the air of dales farmer, Dan was expecting to be told 'get off my land' at any moment.

Detective Chief Inspector David Shaw was the most Yorkshire of Yorkshiremen Dan had ever met, they sat and went through the case notes to the John Carter murder. DCI Shaw gave the impression of being a blundering oaf, but he did more listening than talking and when he asked questions they were incisive and directly to the point. Dan talked the DCI through the events surrounding the murder, he voiced his concerns over Judith Carter's arrest and pointed out the coincidence of Josh Filmore's death. The DCI told Dan off for interfering with someone else's case and interfering with a Home Office Pathologist, then slapped him on the back and said "but, the rest is some bloody good work lad".

Dan emerged from the DCI's office drained late in the afternoon, most people including Naz had left for home. But, she had left a couple of post-it notes on his screen 'phone US embassy' and 'B phoned'. Dan found a number for the US embassy on the internet and phoned it, "hello this is detective sergeant Cawood" and before he could finish a very efficient American voice on the other end of the phone said "hello sergeant the deputy ambassador is waiting for your call I'll put you through" now Dan was confused. Then a smooth Californian accent spoke and Dan understood "hello sergeant sorry to bother you at work I'm Josh Filmore's father and my son spoke of you in his last telephone call to his mother, I was hoping you could give me some of your time to help me work out what happened to my son". Dan could hear the sadness in the man's voice and felt sorry for him.

They talked for half an hour Dan tried to answer questions without compromising the murder case. Against his better judgement Dan agreed to meet Jon Filmore at the weekend and take him on to the moors around Robin Hood's Bay. Dan felt drained by the call to Jon Filmore but took out his mobile and phoned Bea back "good afternoon major, I've got something for you why don't you pop round to the house for supper" and with that Dan was looking forward to a night of good food, good whisky and better company.

Dan set off for home he walked quickly stopping only at the off licence to get a bottle of Lagavulin. He showered and sang at the top of his voice to a couple of Iron Maiden tracks before putting on his leathers and heading off to Bea's.

Dan arrived at Bea's he was invited in like the old friend he was. Bea and Dan sat in the garden watching the sun set drinking whisky and smoking their pipes while Tim made supper. It was late by the time they ate and everyone had had a drink, they talked ate and drank some more and by the time they all went to bed at 2am the world was a better place. Dan had just striped off and was climbing into bed when Bea knocked on his door and entered. "You forgot your package Major" she said threw a brown paper package on the bed wished him good night and left.

Dan got a second wind and was instantly awake, he sat up and opened the package it was a copy of Josh Filmore's autopsy notes. Dan flicked through them until he found Bea's conclusions. There was evidence of a pre-mortem struggle with bruising around Josh's neck and damage to his finger nails where he had scratched someone, but no DNA evidence under the fingernails Bea guessed it had been washed away by the sea or the struggle could have taken place many hours before death. As the cause of death was multiple blunt force trauma, resulting in multiple injury including a broken neck, all symptomatic of a high fall. There were further blunt force trauma injuries, cuts and abrasions that were post-mortem, Bea guessed most likely caused by the action of the tide pounding the body against the cliffs.

Dan spent hours thinking, turning the events of the last couple of weeks over inside his head, before he eventually turned his light out and went to sleep as the sun was coming up.

Fell Walker by Peter Rankin © 2023

Chapter Twenty One – Bingo

Bea's housekeeper knocked on Dan's door and woke him at 6:30am "Come in" said Dan. She put a tray with a full English, a mug of tea and a copy of the Times on the end of Dan's bed and said "nice to see you Major" as she opened the curtains. "Nice to be seen, how are you Doreen?" enquired Dan "Oh Fine, you know a bit of arthritis but other than that fine" she said.

Doreen had been the nanny to Bea's children, she had never married and over the years had become a member of the family, gradually becoming a housekeeper as the children left home. She was now in her seventies and lived in the old game keeper's cottage at the entrance to the house. Bea had tried many times over the years to get her to take it easy and retire, but Doreen said she liked to work it kept her young.

Doreen sat on the end of Dan's bed she talked while he ate "I was sorry to hear about your divorce, but you'll be alright a good looking lad like you with plenty of prospects. You'll have the girls fighting over you" she said. Dan laughed out loud he liked her optimism "I'm nearly forty, I've just retired from any good prospects I was ever going to have and I'm a bald and scarred but other that Doreen you got it spot on" he said.

After breakfast Dan dressed and went downstairs he sat with Tim and Bea, had a cup of tea and thanked them for their hospitality. He kissed Bea on the check to say good-bye and whispered "thanks, I owe you one" and left for work.

For once Dan wasn't the first at work he arrived just before DI King still wearing the clothes he had on last night, a t-shirt and a pair of shorts. He quickly changed in to the clothes he kept under his desk for emergencies and then had a cup of tea with Naz. It was Tuesday and she had bought a copy of Heat so they sat for twenty minutes and pawed over the pictures celebrity gossip.

Dan wanted to return to the Maguire's he had some statements that needed signing and wanted a full inventory of stolen goods for his files. So Naz took a car from the car pool and they drove over to Knapton.

Dan pulled up outside the house there was a supermarket van delivering groceries outside. Dan and Naz went into the house and were made a cup of tea. "So how did you e-mail in your order, I thought your laptop was stolen?" asked Dan as he pointed to the bags of groceries in the hall, "Oh we're lazy we just have the same order every week, we just cancelled it while we were on holiday" said Peter Maguire.

Dan got the list of stolen goods and his statements signed, gave the Maguire's their crime reference number made his excuses and left as fast as he could. "What's the big rush?" asked Naz as they sped back towards the station. "Do you remember Shannon Davis, she was doing her shopping on-line when we went to see her, we might just have found our common thread" said Dan and even though he was driving gave a little dance.

Once back at the station they phoned all the victims of burglary and sure enough every one of them usually bought their groceries on-line. With the last phone call made Dan looked at Naz and said "Bingo!". Naz and Dan grabbed a sandwich from the canteen for lunch and headed for the local supermarket. They arrived and went to reception Dan knew how quickly gossip went round a place of work like a supermarket, so introduced himself as Major Danton Cawood, showed his military ID and asked to see the manager. The last thing he wanted was the burglar getting wind of his presence and doing a runner.

Dan and Naz were escorted to an office where they were given tea and biscuits and waited thirty minutes for an assistant manager to arrive. "I'm sorry for the subterfuge" said Dan "but I'm DS Cawood and this is DC Bush, we wanted to make a low profile entry and I really do need to speak to the manager". This time it only took a few seconds and the manager arrived. Dan spoke as soon as he entered "I'm sorry to tell you this Mr Robson, but there have been a spate of burglaries in the York area throughout the summer you may have read about them in the evening press. We have found that every one of the victims had their groceries delivered by your on-line service and every one of the victims cancelled their delivery for two weeks during which time the crimes took place". Mr Robson sat down and said "Oh! Fuck".

Mr Robson was more than accommodating, his main concern was to keep the matter under wraps. The assistant manager in charge of on-line orders and the personnel manager were brought in along with sandwiches and drinks, While Mr Robson contacted head office and the supermarket solicitors to find his legal position and what he was allowed do and what he was not. "Well sergeant I've spoken to my boss and he wants me to give you as much help as I can without breaking the law, a company solicitor is on the way now and she's a specialist in dealing with the Data Protection Act. I've also got the press team from head office on their way here and if this anything to do with us I hope you'll work with us on breaking the story to the press".

They sat in the office while Freya the on-line manager explained the process of getting orders out to people's houses. An order was taken on-line and the money transfer processed by head office, these orders were then sent to the local branch with an on-line shop and was printed out by one of the admin assistants. They made up a picking order for the warehouse staff to put together and bag the shopping. The order was then put in the back of a refrigerated van ready for delivery. Between managers, admin staff, pickers and drivers it was nearly thirty people working seven days a week. "So who knows about regular orders and whether they would be cancelled?" asked Dan, "Oh! Just me and my admin team" said Freya.

"OK lets start with them" said Dan, "how closely do you work with these admin people?" asked Naz, "we all work in an open plan office there's only me and three of them" said Freya. "Have you noticed if any of your team have bought nice clothes, shoes, new bags anything like that recently?" enquired Naz, "well Judy has just had a birthday and her boyfriend bought her a pair of Jimmy Choo's" said Freya with an air of Jealousy. "Expensive?" said Dan "£400 for a pair of shoes" said Naz. "Bloody Hell" said Dan and Mr Robson in unison.

With that Judy Smith's personnel file was brought in Naz radioed through to the station for a quick check of the files. After a few minutes the report came back, she had just turned eighteen but had multiple juvenile shop lifting convictions in Selby dating back over the last three years that she hadn't mentioned on her job application form. It was Judy's day off so Dan took her details and He and Naz drove out to her house. Leaving

Mr Robson to go through the other personnel files of everyone involved in on-line shopping.

Naz and Dan drove to the address on her personnel file, the same one given on her Police file. It was a small bed-sit in a large block just off Walmgate in the centre of town. The block was run by a housing association, and the bottom of the stairs were blocked with prams and two skinny adolescents who wanted to know if Dan had the price of a cuppa. They climbed the stairs to the flat and knocked on the door, there was no answer.

They waited a few minutes Dan put on a pair of latex gloves and took out his lock picks from his pocket. He had been given a magic set for his eleventh birthday by his mother, he hated it, but had started him on lock picking. Then when Dan had worked on a surveillance team in Northern Ireland for six months he used to try and pick locks to pass the time. It was a fairly simple three tumbler lock, and Dan found the movements one by one slipping in three picks and then twisted. There was a slight grating noise and a click as the door opened.

Dan pushed on the door, there was something preventing it from opening, a pile of letters. Dan and then Naz squeezed into the single room flat it obviously hadn't been lived in for weeks and there was nothing of worth in the flat so they left and returned to the supermarket.

Back at the supermarket Dan spoke to the manager, he had been through all the other personnel files from on-line shopping and couldn't see anything strange. Judy Smith was at work at 6am the following morning and Naz and Dan would be there waiting when she arrived. They left and drove back to the station.

Dan tidied his paperwork up and left for home it was getting late and after a weekend of drinking followed by a night at Bea's Dan was knackered. He stopped at M & S on his way home and bought some proper food. Dan made himself an omelette and wrote up his case diary before falling a sleep in front of the TV.

Fell Walker by Peter Rankin © 2023

Chapter Twenty Two - A little IT Problem

Dan was woken by his alarm clock at 4am he showered and dressed, leaving the flat on his bike without having breakfast. He arrived at the supermarket just before 5am at first light. The manager was there already he was waiting with a team of suits from head office. Mr Robson and Dan waited in his office eating bacon sandwiches and drinking tea. He was a nice bloke and they chatted about this and that for a while, Mr Robson was Dan's age and came from York. But, in his suit and office carrying around an extra 60 pounds and the stress of not meeting targets set by head office Dan thought he looked in his fifties.

Naz arrived just before 6 and they all waited quietly in Mr Robson's office until Judy Smith was due to turn up for work in ten minutes. It was getting quite full in the office there was Naz, Dan , Mr Robson, a press agent from head office, a team of solicitors from head office and two assistant managers, it was now standing room only. "Look" said Dan "we can't ask Miss Smith any questions with the room so full, I am either going to talk to her by myself here or take her down to the station", "I'd like to stay" said one of the legal team "I'm here to act as Miss Smith's solicitor", "If that's OK with her it's OK with me" said Dan. Everyone left but Dan, Naz, Mr Robson and the solicitor.

Fell Walker by Peter Rankin © 2023

A couple of minutes later the phone rang "Thanks Angela if you could just show her in" said Mr Robson. A couple of seconds later in walked Judy Smith she was a frail sickly looking young woman barely more than school age. Mr Robson spoke "Judy you've been asked to come to my office to speak with the police this is detective sergeant Cawood and the is detective constable Bush", "hello Judy" said Dan as he showed her his warrant card "we need to ask you some questions about a number of burglaries that have taken place around York over the last couple of months" as Dan mentioned burglaries Judy began to cry and Dan felt like a bastard but carried on. "Judy there are some rights you need to be aware of before we go any further, first of all Mr Robson and Mr?" "Willis" said the solicitor and let Dan carry on "are here to help you out, Mr Willis has been hired by the store to act as your legal representative and Mr Robson would like to know what happened so he can put things right, if you want either of them to leave just say so".

Judy sobbed "no that's OK, they're alright" and Dan told Judy her rights then checked his hankie was clean and gave it to her. Judy had a slight West Riding accent Dan couldn't place. "I gave the addresses to Steven it was his idea, we were only going to do it once to get a deposit for a flat, and now if we stop they're gonna kill him" said Judy. "Who's Steven?" said Dan "we grew up together in Oakfield's in Selby" said Judy, "Is

Oakfield's a children's home?" said Dan, "yeah we both got kicked out last year when we were seventeen" replied Judy. "Did you get the flat Judy?" asked Dan "yeah" she whimpered. "Is Steven there now?" asked Dan "yeah" another whimper. Dan found out the address and left the room to go to the toilet.

Once in the loo he made a phone call "Mum, listen I'm just about to arrest an eighteen year old girl who's homeless, she's the saddest thing you've ever seen. If you're still in contact with that women's refuge the one with the solicitor then you need to get down to the station and get this girl bailed and into the refuge 'cos a night in the cells will kill her". With that Dan hung up and returned to the office.

Dan explained to Judy that she was going to be arrested and must wait in the office with Naz for a few minutes. He went outside with the store manager and the suits from head office. They all agreed that Judy was no master criminal and they all agreed that it was in everyone's best interest if the stores involvement in the case was kept under wraps for now.

Naz and Dan drove a sobbing Judy to the station once there she was charged and processed. Her fingerprints and DNA taken, then she was taken down to the cells. Within minutes though her solicitor arrived not a grey man in a grey suit, but a beautiful woman in an elegant dress.

Fell Walker by Peter Rankin © 2023

Dan went to see the DCI and told him about the progress on the case and was given the green light to bring in Steven Richards.

Chapter Twenty Three – Cutting Remarks

Dan checked Steven Richards record on the computer, he had a long list of petty crimes to his name mostly as a juvenile burglary, shop lifting, handling stolen goods and possession of cannabis. Meanwhile Naz signed out a car from the garage. They drove into the Bell farm estate, a small run down council estate just out of town, they found Steven Richards flat and drove round the block that contained it. It was a post war brick built block of flats, with open stairwells and walkways Richards flat was on the second floor with the only access being through the front door.

They sat in the car and prepared to make an arrest, Naz asked if she could have the collar and Dan thought it would be good experience. They watched the flat for 30 minutes there was no signs of unusual activity so they moved in for the kill. They climbed the stairs with Naz in front and arrived at the door to flat 42. The whole place looked like it had had a lot of money spent on it only to remain in a state of decay and neglect. Dan thought of council estates in much the same way as he thought of the NHS, they could always swallow more money and needed someone to care not a whole new set of government initiatives.

The door to flat 42 was a new uPVC door but it had already suffered from a fire and was charred and misshaped from melting. Naz rang the bell but there was no noise, so Dan reached over her shoulder and banged on the door. After just a few seconds a thin dirty looking face appeared that Dan recognised from his record, it was Steven Richards he was wearing a track suit and trainers that were very dirty he had opened the door with his right hand but his left arm was held behind his body.

Naz held out her warrant card and said "Hello Mr. Richards I'm DC Bush and this is DS Cawood of the North Yorkshire Police would you mind if we come in please", "no problems, what's this about?" enquired Richards and opened the door up fully. Naz stepped across the threshold and was just about to answer when Richards Slammed the door as hard as he could trapping her between the door and the frame, then slashed at her arm with whatever was in his left hand.

Dan rocked backwards then charged through the door, he weighed more than the other two put together. Richards had been pushed back and was unsteady on feet, but Naz was sent sprawling on the hall floor and Dan had to pull himself back to stop himself stomping Naz's body. Richards needed to get past Dan if he was going to escape so he charged him and raked Dan's chest with his fists.

Dan looked down he could see Naz in a pool of blood and blood all over his chest and stomach. He stepped over her while blows were being rained down up his chest and shoulders and swiped an almighty bear like swipe with his right arm. It wasn't any move you might see at a boxing match, but it carried Dan's full weight and all of his strength. It caught Richards just under his ribs on his left side, lifted him completely off his feet and carried him about 7 feet before slamming him into the hall wall. Richards slid down the wall and landed spread eagle on the floor, Dan dived forwards and landed with his elbows out on Richards' rib cage. Dan heard an almighty crack and knew he had done enough damage to immobilise him.

Dan pushed himself up and looked around, Steven Richards was sobbing and wheezing on the floor while holding onto his chest. Naz was dazed and confused she was lying on the floor in a pool of blood trying but failing to stand her self up. Finally Dan looked down at himself his shirt had several cuts down the front and was covered in blood. He opened it and saw multiple slash wounds down this right shoulder and across his chest. Dan stood, he took a pair of latex gloves from his pocket and put them on. He opened each of the wounds on his chest one by one whilst breathing heavily, there was no bubbling so he knew his chest cavity was intact but he also knew he was losing a lot of blood.

Dan stepped over Richards and found the kitchen, he opened the cupboards and drawers and pulled out their contents onto the floor until he found a roll of cling film. Dan took his shirt off and wrapped the cling film as tightly as he could around his left shoulder and chest. He put on multiple layers until the bleeding began to subside.

Next Dan phoned the station he told them what had happened and asked for two ambulances, some uniform officers and Jimmy Garner. Then he went back into the hall and checked on Naz, she had managed to sit herself up but was concussed and her arm was streaming with blood. Dan ripped the right arm off her blouse and wrapped it in cling film again tight until the blood flow reduced to a trickle. Dan checked Naz's pulse and watched her rib cage as she breathed. Her pulse was high but not excessively given what had just happened and her breathing seemed regular.

Finally Dan moved over to Richards he was curled up in a ball now, but still wheezing and sobbing. Dan could also see there was blood at the corner of his mouth. The last thing Dan wanted was to get any type of blood infection, one of his sergeants in Belfast had contracted Hepatitis when he was a passer by at a car accident and had stopped to help, it was a lesson Dan would never forget.

Dan stood over Richards he reckoned a broken rib and a collapsed lung, he would be in pain but a short stay in hospital would see the lung re-inflated. There was lots of blood over his tracksuit but no obvious cuts, Dan assumed it must have been transfer from either Naz or himself. Just next to Richards on the floor was a Stanley knife, the blade looked a bit old and rusty "Shit" said Dan to himself when he realised he would have to have a tetanus jab. Dan tore off a few feet of cling film and carefully picked the knife up and put it on a shelf.

There was a knock at the door, it was a paramedic on a bike he'd been passing the end of the street when the call came through. Dan introduced himself. Then he gloved up and quickly examined Naz and Richards. Within minutes he was on the radio Richards had at least two broken ribs and a punctured lung, Naz was concussed with superficial wounds. The paramedic having put both Naz and Richards in the recovery position could do nothing more until the ambulance arrived, so he began to examine Dan's chest.

He took the cling film off carefully and a couple of the compressed wounds began to bleed heavily. "Bloody Hell" said the paramedic as he carefully probed Dan's chest "these two deep ones need stitches". "OK" said Dan "get on with it". The paramedic cleaned then began stitching the two deep wounds on Dan's chest, it really bloody hurt and Dan shouted out in pain but didn't move. It wasn't the first time he'd been stitched up without anaesthetic and doubted it would be the last.

While Dan was attended to ambulances, police cars and the DCI all arrived. Dan was stopping people entering the flat just letting the ambulance crew in to take away Naz and Richards with a police escort. The paramedic had patched Dan up the best he could but Dan was still in pain and bleeding. He was just explaining to the DCI what had happened when Jimmy Garner turned up. Jimmy wanted Dan's clothes and brought him his wellies and a paper over suit to get changed into.

It was Jimmy's scene now and he didn't want anyone in the flat unless they were suited up and sterile. Dan didn't want to leave the scene so he stripped naked outside the flat and got changed. Jimmy spent half an hour taking photos and documenting the crime scene. The spare room was full of electronic goods, jewellery and other stolen goods. Richards must have been decorating with his new found wealth, Jimmy thought he had been laying a new carpet when Naz and Dan arrived, 'that would explain the knife' thought Dan.

Eventually after nearly an hour on scene the DCI took Dan to one side and ordered him to the hospital. Dan was driven to the local A&E department by uniform and saw the doctor. He was happy with most of the paramedics work, but put a couple of stitches in Dan's shoulder just to be on the safe side and of course gave him a tetanus jab.

Dan phoned his mum and asked her to bring him in some clothes. As soon as he'd put the phone down he regretted it. Within 10 minutes a blur of hair, purple dress, tears and worry came running into the waiting room and hugged him. Dan held himself in check but gently pushed his mother away as he pointed out the fresh blood on his shoulder through the bandage where she'd popped the stitches.

Once Dan had changed and calmed his mum down he went off to the wards to see Naz, Ian had already arrived and was sat holding her hand. Naz had some stitches on her right shoulder and was still a little unsteady and dizzy so was staying in overnight for observation. She had a huge lump and bruise where her head had smashed into the wall, but luckily there was no permanent damage to her face.

Ian was more shocked about the whole thing than anyone else, all Naz really cared about was that it was her collar and she wanted to be back on duty when Richards was arrested. Dan said he would go and find out what was happening to him. Dan found Richards under police guard, he had two broken ribs and a collapsed lung, but luckily his lung hadn't been punctured. The blood in his mouth had been from his smashed front teeth, where his face had been smashed into the wall. Richards' doctor said there was nothing he could do for the ribs other than strap them up and the collapsed lung would be re-inflated within 24 hours. The on call dentist was coming to see him later this afternoon, but he reckoned Richards should be released the day after tomorrow.

Dan returned to see Naz and told her she would need to be at work on Friday if she wanted the collar, wished her all the best and set off for the station. Dan walked home, changed then walked into work. He was back at his desk by 4:30pm typing up a report on the incident earlier today. DCI Shaw walked through the Incident room stopped and said "what the bloody hell do you think you're doing here?" he was annoyed at Dan for not being fit for work, he sent him home and said he didn't want to see him until Friday at the earliest.

Dan walked home he stopped in town for a drink. He stood at the bar of the Bluebell Inn a tiny little pub that hadn't changed in over a hundred years both inside and out, and drank a few pints of real ale whilst he smoked his pipe. By the time Dan got home it was 9:30pm the combination of the beer, no food since breakfast and the loss of blood had made him a little drunk and unsteady on his feet. He walked into the bedroom and collapsed on the bed.

Chapter Twenty Four – A Day of Rest

Dan woke late it was 9am, his head was just a dull ache and his body a mass of sharp pain. Normally he would stand in the shower for an age until he began to feel human again, but he wasn't allowed to get his wound dressings wet. So he dug round in the drawers until he found some Nurofen, took 3 and washed them down with a cup of tea. Then he sat down and wrote what he should have written down last night, the days notes for the holiday burglaries diary.

Once dressed Dan went to the shop, and returned to make himself poached eggs on toast for breakfast. It was the only food he could face when he was feeling ill. Dan sat in front of the telly and watched an hour of daytime rubbish.

Then he went upstairs to see his mum, she sat him down and fussed around him. Dan hated being fussed over but sat in his mum's sitting room, drinking herbal tea and wrapped in a lama wool blanket. He knew he was loved unconditionally by at least one person in the world and in his delicate state both physically and emotionally that was important. Dan spent the rest of the morning drifting in and out of sleep on the sofa letting whatever his mum was saying wash over him like another blanket.

Fell Walker by Peter Rankin © 2023

Dan and his mum took the dog for a walk by the river, they chatted about his cases not in any great detail and his mum's latest causes. Once back at the house his mum had her yoga group coming round so Dan decided to go and see Naz and find out how she was doing.

He walked down to the hospital bought a bunch of white roses his favourite flower and went upstairs to see Naz. She was surrounded by friends and family, Dan was introduced but felt out of place. Naz was a well loved person and her father repeatedly told her "being a policeman was no job for a lady". To which she would reply with a smile "but Daddy someone's got to make the tea". Her father must have been over sixty but he was a good looking regal gentleman with thick well groomed hair. Dan felt a little under dressed in his shorts and 'hard rock café. New York' t-shirt. Naz was going to be released later in the afternoon and wanted to be in work tomorrow to interview Richards, so Dan left wondering who would come and surround his hospital bed with love.

On his way out of the hospital he stopped at the chemist and bought enough plasters and bandages to equip a small field hospital. Then he turned round and went back upstairs to see Steven Richards. There was a uniform PC sat outside his private room 'who said crime doesn't pay' thought Dan. He flashed his warrant card and went in.

"Hello Steven I'm DS Cawood" said Dan, Richards looked in shook and said "I'm really sorry I didn't mean to cut you up, I just had a knife in my hand" "I know Steven, you were laying your carpet there was a knock at the door, you had a tool in you hand and you panicked. Then in a moment of madness you slashed out at two police officers in a bid to escape" said Dan "yeah, yeah that's it honest mate" said Richards. "How are you?" said Dan and pointed to the chest drain by his bed, "they're gonna release me tomorrow my lung's better and the dentist has taken my teeth out" said Richards as he lifted his lip with his finger to show where two premolars had been removed. There were tears in his eyes and Dan looked at him objectively for the first time, he was a scrawny lad of 18 who had got in way over his head. He had moved from petty theft to semi-organised crime without thinking about it, he wouldn't last a week in prison. "listen Steven" said Dan "I'm going to offer you a deal, but this is unofficial you're going to have to trust me. You've knifed a copper and put her in hospital there's no way the CPS isn't going to want to prosecute you for GBH. You've burgled and stolen people's identities and with your record that means you're going down for a long stretch. I'm not being funny but you won't survive a day in Armley, you'll be in and out of the doctor's office having your arse stitched up".

Richards looked in despair "so what do you want" he said in a whimper, "I want the people who you sold on the goods to. The people who told you how to steal identities" said Dan. "What do I get?" replied Richards chirping up a bit, "you get me" said Dan "when this goes to court I'll stand up for you, I'll tell the beak just what I've said to you and I'll tell him just how much you've helped in catching the people behind the identity theft ring". "If I grass they'll fuckin' kill me in prison, you fuckin' know they will" said Richards, "If you grass I'll have a word with the CPS, and recommend to the magistrate if asked that you don't get a custodial sentence" said Dan then turned to leave but added "think about it, it's the best offer you're going to get. I'll see you tomorrow". As Dan turned to walk out Richards said "Mr Cawood is Jude OK she's not really up for this kind of thing", "she's fine no thanks to you though" said Dan and left

On his way out Dan spoke to the PC on duty and asked him to make sure no-one saw the prisoner and that he didn't have access to phone. Jimmy Garner had taken away Richards clothes but there was still some of his personal effects in a bag with the PC. Dan got a pen and a piece of paper from the nurses station and spent the next quarter of an hour copying down all the contacts in Richards phone and a list of calls received. Unfortunately Richards had deleted all his text messages so Dan left to go home.

Dan began to walk home but his mind drifted off and before he knew it he was in the middle of the city centre standing not knowing where he was or where he was going. He phoned his mum "come on do you want to try Betty's again, and this time I promise I'm off duty". Dan met his mum at Betty's they were treated like royalty, taken out of the queue as soon as they were recognised. They were given a great table in the window where they could people watch all the tourists and shoppers passing by. The manager came over thanked Dan and gave his mum a complimentary bottle of wine as Dan insisted that he couldn't take anything because he was just doing his job. Dan's mum complained that she didn't like being made a fuss of, but Dan could see the beaming smile on her face every time one of the staff smiled knowingly at them.

After tea Dan walked his mum home they sat on her sofa, drank whisky and put the world to rights. Dan eventually slid downstairs to bed at midnight.

Chapter Twenty Five – Good Cop Bad Cop

Dan woke up at 5am he felt rested in both body and spirit, there was still some pain in his shoulder and chest but other than that he felt great. He showered took a photo of his stitches and changed the dressings on his shoulder then sat down to check his e-mails. There was the usual mix of messages from the AK-47 club, Dan uploaded the photo of his shoulder to his computer then e-mailed it to all the other members of the club, another tradition.

The club's members were currently spread out across the world and although they only met once in a blue moon, they were the only people Dan could call friends. There were photos of bombings, bullet riddled buildings and John 'Jack' Ladier sent him a picture of an enormous tropical ulcer he had on his leg. There was an e-mail from the General he would be in the UK next year for an inspection visit to one of the USAF bases, 'will that man never retire' thought Dan. Dan e-mailed back perhaps he would have a chance to give the General the present he had had for him for nearly twenty years, but never got the chance.

'will you be travelling on military transport and if so do you still have friends in the military who owe you a favour?' wrote Dan knowing that the answer would be 'once a general in US air force always a general in the US air force.'

Fell Walker by Peter Rankin © 2023

Dan made himself a bacon and tomato sandwich and washed it down with a mug of strong tea, then dressed and set off for work. As usual he was the first in the incident room, while he waited for Naz to arrive he studied the John Carter murder white board. There were crime scene photos, a time line and Judith Carter's photograph. The case had been reopened and links with the Josh Filmore murder examined but Judith Carter remained in Jail. At 7:30 the DCI arrived "bloody hell Cawood, have you a home to go to" he said then they had a cuppa and discussed what was happening with the holiday break-ins. Dan told him they had a potential way in on an identity theft ring, the fraud squad were interested and the DCI said he would contact the CPS to see if a deal could be made.

Naz arrived a little after 8am she had a black eye and her arm was in a sling, but she also had a twinkle in her eye and was talking the quick excited talk of someone desperate to get on with things. It would be her first major interview taking the lead, Dan was happy for her and also thought it would be good experience as there was little she could do to cock it up.

One by one the detectives arrived, walking into the incident room each wearing their stab vest and a smile, making a point of walking over to say good morning to Naz and Dan. Eventually last through the door was DI King in his stab vest at bang on 8:30am. He walked past their desk and just winked while he rubbed his vest between his thumb and forefinger.

Once all the ribbing had stopped mainly because DC 'Johno' Wheeler came over to ask "does that hurt?" pointed at Naz's black eye and promptly stuck his finger in her eye by accident. There was a huge communal "ooh!" from everyone in the incident room and profound apologies from DC Wheeler and with that everyone returned to their work.

Dan phoned DC Khan told him that they would be interviewing Richards this afternoon if he was released from hospital. Dan invited him to sit in on the interview and was happy to offer Richards a deal and get the info DC Khan wanted, so long as Naz and Dan were part of any subsequent arrest. DC Khan came down to the incident room and all three of them sat down and discussed what information they wanted from Richards. DC Feroz Khan was slightly shorter than Dan, but was still a tall, slim, handsome, athletic, good looking young man, Dan thought he and Naz made quite the pair. Feroz known around the station as 'Fez' was quick witted, with a dark sense of humour Dan liked him. He had a pronounced English accent with every so often a hint of a Pakistani accent and Dan guessed his grandparents had moved to the UK many years ago.

Fell Walker by Peter Rankin © 2023

All three of them ate lunch together, Dan liked the station despite being built in the 70s, it still had a lot of tradition that dated back to when the police thought of themselves as a force nicking villains not a service ensuring good performance to their customers. Here on Friday it was always fish and chips, one of the police vans would disappear down to the local chippie at about 11:30, returning at 12noon with one of each for 30 hungry coppers. Even Naz had deep fried food on a Friday. Fish, chips, mushy peas and a mug of tea followed by a well planned good cop, bad cop interview. Dan felt like he should have a bottle of cheap whisky in his desk and go and pick Richards up in a MK 1 Ford Granada.

After fish and chips Dan phoned the hospital to discover that Richards had seen the Consultant and was ready for release. It was decided that DC Khan and Dan would pick Richards up while Naz prepared for the interview. They took a car from the motor pool and headed off to the hospital. Once there Dan went upstairs to the ward to find Richards still in bed in his private room. Dan couldn't resist it he was having a good day looked at Richards and said "put your clothes on, your nicked". Richards who was way too young to have ever seen Jack Reagan in full flight just looked on confused as Dan left his room with a big grin on his face. Half an hour later Richards was dressed in a boiler suit and sat in the back of a ford focus on his way to the station.

On arrival at the Police Station there was still all the paperwork to do. Richards was taken through the custody suite, he was charged and told his rights, before being lead off to see the police doctor to make sure he was fit for an interview. There was more delay when Richards asked to see a solicitor before going in to interview. By the time Naz, DC Khan, Dan, the duty solicitor and Richards sat down in a room together it was 5pm. By that time the DCI had been in touch with the CPS they had the go ahead to offer Richards a deal. DC Khan's boss had been down to see them, he wanted a result from the Richards interview if nothing else it would be good PR.

Naz did most of the talking she told Richards his rights again, explained the interview procedure and that the tape was there for everyone's protection. She explained that DC Khan was there purely as an observer and wouldn't be taking part in the interview. She went through the case against Richards, Naz was being ruthless she spoke like an automaton and brought out enough evidence to him down for a long time. She showed him photos of crime scenes and the stolen goods in his flat. She showed him the DNA match between himself and that found on a blood sample taken from broken glass at one of the crime scenes. She read the statement made by Judy Smith only two days earlier. She brought out the Stanley knife wrapped in a plastic bag and put it on the desk then finally she lifted the bandage on her arm and showed him the stitches he had caused. "Look I going to make sure you go down for as long possible" said Naz and for the first time shrank back into her chair and then started crying. Everyone including Dan looked confused.

"I'm sure the magistrate won't be lenient when I've told him how you rushed at me with a knife, I thought you were going to kill me" Naz sniffled showing Richards just how she would act in the witness box 'clever girl' thought Dan. Richards looked stunned then whispered something to his solicitor. "OK, what do you want and what will my client get" said the solicitor.

"We want to know who put you up to the identity theft and where those details are now. We want to know who fenced all your stolen goods and we want to know who did the break-ins with you" said Naz back in her no nonsense madam mode. There was a long pause and then "You get GBH, assault with a deadly weapon and resisting arrest reduced to common assault, you get the identity theft charges dropped and if we get a result from your intel, you get a recommendation to the magistrate that a custodial sentence wouldn't be appropriate in your case" said Dan in much more friendly manner.

There was a brief conversation in whispers between Richards and his solicitor "OK, you've got a deal" said the solicitor. The interview was suspended while Dan went outside and made everyone a cup of tea. On his return he got the full story. Richards and Judy Smith had come up with the idea of burgling her absent clients when they were drunk about six months ago. Richards had burgled a couple of houses by himself while Judy was at work, then sold the gear on e-bay. But, the money trickled through and he wanted instant cash, the third burglary had nearly gone wrong he was leaving through the back door as the next door neighbour was coming in through the front door to feed the cat. The goods from that burglary he took over to Leeds on the train, and sold in a second hand shop in Chapel Allerton. He had seen their advert in the Yorkshire Post when looking through the vacancies page at the Job Centre 'DVDs bought for Cash'. Once there Richards got talking to the shop keeper, he was the one who suggested stealing identities and that he could put him in touch with a man who would buy the information.

So a couple of days later Richards went back to Chapel Allerton and Met 'Robbo', he didn't know his real name but he knew his cell phone number and where he lived. Richards guessed that 'Robbo' was in his late forties and described him as a pit bull covered in Leeds United tattoos. 'Robbo' had told Richards what he needed to get some cash out of identities, and the rest of burglaries had been done with one of Robbo's mates Jamie. Again Richards didn't know Jamie's real name but he knew his cell phone number and that he drove a clapped out blue Peugeot van.

Jamie had been the one who decided which houses to burgle, they would spend a day driving around York looking at empty houses and the next day on the job. Jamie always tried to pick out of the way houses with gardens that weren't overlooked. He was a seasoned pro, he knew how to get in, where the valuables would be and had nerves of steel, twice returning to the scene to pick up credit cards they had applied for in the victims' name. When the burglaries became more frequent Judy got concerned, but after a visit from Robbo she was shown the error of her ways. Jamie was due to come over to the flat next Tuesday and do a recce of a few houses they knew would be empty, and hopefully they would be on the job on Wednesday. Richards was now reduced to the role of driver and look out, he drove Jamie and his friends to the houses and acted as look out. Richards had been told by Jamie and Robbo that this was a job life and if wanted out of the job he wanted out of life as well.

Fell Walker by Peter Rankin © 2023

By the time the interview was over it was getting on for 7pm Dan was happy to see the two DCs working well together, so made his excuses and left the paperwork and sorting out to Naz and DC Khan. She was really enjoying doing some proper police work and not just making tea for DI King, Dan was really happy for her. He liked Naz and she had the makings of a good copper. Dan wanted to give her some responsibility and make her feel like she was making a difference, it was the only way she was going to get confidence in her own abilities. Anyway Dan thought 'I'll have an hour in work on Monday before she arrives to check the paperwork'.

Dan walked home as quickly as he could. Once home he showered, changed and wrote notes in the case diary for the 'holiday burglaries' he had only just put his pen down when his phone rang. "Hi there, it's Jon Filmore I'm at the railway station, I've booked a room at the Dean Court Hotel. I know I'm not supposed to be here until tomorrow, but I was hoping we could meet".

The hotel was just around the corner from Dan's flat so he agreed to meet Josh's father for Dinner, Dan knew the food would be nice but wasn't looking forward to the company and it also meant putting on long trousers.

Dan met Jon Filmore in the pubic bar of the Dean Court, they sat and had a drink while weighing each other up. Josh had been a chip off the old block Jon was tall and athletically slim only no wild hair, he must have been 5 or six years older than Dan but time had been kind to him. He spoke with a melodic Californian accent and instantly put Dan at ease. He was well dressed but his fine suit and open neck shirt gave an air informality. Dan shouldn't have been surprised that a diplomat gave a great first impression.

Jon and Dan sat down to dinner, eventually the talk turned to Josh. Dan told Jon how his son had spent the last few weeks of his life making friends and entertaining people with his quiet but easy going sense of humour, reassuring everyone that if half starved Yank could walk 20 miles then full blooded Englishmen should have no problems. Jon told Dan that he lived out his last few days the way he had lived his whole life. They talked about the coast to coast walk, they talked about Dan's cottage in the Bay, they talked about Josh's childhood, but what they didn't talk about was Josh's death.

Jon wanted to see where Josh had spent his last few happy days. So they agreed that tomorrow Jon would hire a car and the two of them would drive over to the Bay and spend the night in the cottage. Dan left for home not looking forward to a weekend with a grieving father, he was still feeling pretty raw from his divorce and didn't really have it in him to pity anyone else.

Chapter Twenty Six – The Bay

Dan woke at 6am and walked down to the Sainsbury's local to buy some food, he returned home and made himself porridge for breakfast and sat and ate it whilst reading the Times. He went upstairs at 7:30 to tell his mum he would be out for the weekend but she was still asleep, so he took Frisky for a walk down to the river. When he returned he found his mother desperately hung over and searching through the cupboards looking for an aspirin. He gave his mum a kiss and said good-bye, wishing he could stay with her to spend a weekend watching telly drinking whisky and eating an Indian.

Dan went downstairs and packed his bags, he put in his walking boots and waterproofs hoping to at least salvage some fresh air from the weekend. He left the flat and set off for the Dean Court Hotel, on his way he walked down Petergate a street under the shadow of York Minster. The peal of bells announced to the world it was 9am on a gorgeous late summer Saturday in the city, Dan stood and drank in the beauty and warmth of the early morning sun. At the Hotel he found Jon Filmore outside checking over the hire car that had just been delivered. "Morning, are we ready for the off" said Dan.

Fell Walker by Peter Rankin © 2023

Within a few minutes the car was packed and under Dan's direction Jon drove them both towards the coast. At first as they fought their way through early morning traffic the conversation was just a list of instructions from Dan, but within 15 minutes they were on the open road and there was silence in the car.

After about 10 minutes of quiet Jon eventually said "I'm sorry to do this to you this weekend but I want to understand my son and I need to make sense of his death. You don't have to but I'd really like to see where he died" Dan thought about it, if it was his son he'd want to see the spot too. In fact he'd be a pain in the arse to any investigating officer, wanting to know everything that was going on. Dan agreed to take him to the spot, but told him it would be a walk of about 7 miles altogether getting there and back. It turned out that Josh had inherited his love of the outdoors from his father, and Jon was more than happy to get in a bit of walking.

It was decided they would walk from Robin Hood's Bay to Whitby out along the cliff tops looking at the spot where Josh was killed, and return on the in land path along the disused railway track for a well earned meal and a pint in the Dolphin Inn. Before Dan or Jon knew it they were talking about the great outdoors, they talked a lot about the vast open plains of the states. Dan had spent a week with the General every school summer holiday camping, fishing and later on hunting in the great parks of the States and Canada. It turned out that Jon and Dan had both been camping on the edge of Lake George in the summer of 1982.

They talked of the great outdoors across the world, Dan really wanted to go back to Afghanistan when the troubles were over. It was a beautiful country with some wonderful people, but they were suffering from the worst of times. Jon was going to take some time off and go back to New Zealand, he had four years there as the deputy US ambassador when Josh was in High School. They spent most of their spare time in the beautiful unspoilt countryside. New Zealand only had an outdoors laid back culture and the whole country was full of outdoors laid back people.

Jon talked of his other son and his wife, he was distraught and she had flown back to the states to be with him. Jon was staying on in the UK until Josh's body was released by the coroner, then he was going to fly back with the coffin.

They arrived at Robin Hood's Bay just after 11, parked the car and walked down to the cottage. Jon was mesmerised by the charm of the village, wandering down the narrow cobbled streets to the sea front between tiny 200 year old seaman's cottages. Despite being a haven for tourists on this lovely summer's day, the Bay had managed to remain at heart a small seaside community. The trappings of mass tourism hadn't really impacted on the village, not because no-one hadn't tried but because there wasn't any room. There were three pubs, a hand full of tea rooms a sweet shop and a general store none of which would have been out of place in an Enid Blyton book. Dan loved the place for its simplicity, its beauty and its friendliness.

They reached the Dock, where the village met the sea. Jon was taken aback, the village sat in a cleft of rock on the cliffs of the North Yorkshire coast, on the walk down the sea was hidden by the buildings. But. At the bottom of the village the tiny houses opened out on to a majestic bay, surrounded on either side by vast great cliffs that stretched for miles. Then out in front of the village were 'the Scars' long slabs of black rock covered in seaweed that stretched out to the sea at low tide hundreds of yards away. Then beyond was a beautiful calm blue sea, with little bobbing boats at anchor in the bay. All this was framed under a gorgeous summer sky.

They arrived at the cottage Dan felt instantly calmed and at ease, this was his home and the place he felt centred. The cottage was a tall thin house arranged over five floors. There was a basement where Dan stored his army life in packing cases, on the ground floor was a kitchen/diner and a lounge on the first floor. The three bedrooms and two bathrooms were on the

Fell Walker by Peter Rankin © 2023

top two floors and out the back of the cottage was a tiny little yard with a coal bunker and a barbeque. From the bedroom on the top floor was a fantastic sea view that Dan would never tire of waking up to. Although not a big house it was one of the larger cottages in the Bay, but most importantly of all it was where Dan called home.

Jon loved the cottage from the exposed wooden beams, to the uneven floors and the slightly wonky doors. They were all the same things that Dan had fallen in love with so many years ago. Dan's cottage was a bit like him it wasn't tidy and the décor was dated but it had charm and character. The cottage held Dan's life from his army gear in the basement, to his collection of all things nautical scattered all over the house. Dan never threw anything away he just brought it here, there were clothes upstairs that he would have to lose 5 stone to get into. Dan found Jon a pair of wellies to walk in and they set off for Whitby.

They walked out of the village and along the cliff top towards Whitby, after about an hour and a half of walking and chatting they came to the spot where Josh had died. Jon was quiet he studied the rocks then knelt down, made the sign of the cross and said a silent prayer. Dan stood back and watched, his mum still went to church but he had stopped going when he was 16, he wasn't quite sure what he thought of religion.

Fell Walker by Peter Rankin © 2023

Dan took out his pipe and smoked while looking out to sea, it glistened as it reflected the late summer sun.

The coast line undulated up and down with the tall cliffs interspersed with small wooded valleys that carried the rain water off the moors and down to waterfalls over the edge of the cliff. Jon and Dan followed the footpath into one of the small wooded glades, Jon stopped knelt and began to dig a hole. "What are you doing?" enquired Dan, "I'm planting Catalina Ironwood tree seeds, they are native to Catalina Island where Josh and I spent many happy hours". The rest of the journey to Whitby was quiet.

Once in Whitby they walked down to fortune's smokehouse and bought tomorrow's breakfast. They had a cup of tea and a scone in Whitby's old Town then started on the walk home.

The walk followed the line of the old Whitby to Scarborough railway line over the River Esk on a Victorian viaduct and skirting the edge of Farndale moor, whilst still offering great views of the sea. "So we're walking on the fells on the way home" said Jon, "No, no, no not unless we're taking a detour" said Dan as he explained that in the Lake District they called their high uncultivated ground fells. But, here in Yorkshire they were much more sensible choosing to name the lush valleys that had produced so much wealth in centuries gone by. Each wide open valley or

Fell Walker by Peter Rankin © 2023

'Dale' followed a stream or river and was dotted with farms, hamlets and villages. "and if we're really lucky some of those villages have pubs" Dan concluded.

Once back in the Bay Dan showered and changed. They were in the Dolphin Inn eating supper and drinking beer by 8pm. "I know you've done a lot already for me, but I know that Josh was at the scene of a murder just before he died could we go and see the place?" said Jon, without thinking and with a belly full of beer and whisky Dan said "no problems" and regretted it instantly. The rest of the night was spent talking of the John Carter murder. Dan was uncomfortable but again he couldn't help thinking that two murders must somehow be connected.

Dan asked Jon about Josh's money, he didn't know where the £500 in Josh's pocket had come from as he had been working his way around Europe for four months and had never once asked his parents for help. At midnight they helped each other back to the cottage, and Dan collapsed on the bed in his clothes and fell into a deep and restful sleep.

Fell Walker by Peter Rankin © 2023

Chapter Twenty Seven – Hill Walking

Dan woke at 7am with sunlight streaming through his bedroom window, his mouth was dry and his head hurt. He carefully picked his way down three flights of steep stairs to the kitchen, he found an out of date pack of Nurofen took three and drank two pints of water. He sat and felt the heat of the sun through the window while listening to Radio 4, he was listening to the words but his brain wasn't processing the message. After an hour or so Jon came down stairs looking like Dan felt, they were a sorry pair and sat drinking tea.

Dan walked up to the shop and bought a whole host of Sunday papers and a loaf of bread, once back in the cottage he grilled the Fortune's kippers and the cottage was filled with the taste of the sea. Jon and Dan sat quietly drinking tea and eating kippers and toast for breakfast while reading the papers. Every so often one of them would read out loud a funny article and they would both laugh whist holding their heads.

They had a quick walk down along the sea front at low tide and looked for fossils that had been thrown up on the beach by the sea. They walked until they could both face a car journey. Then with a heavy heart Dan locked up the cottage and they left the Bay. The drive to the Lion Inn took longer than Dan expected, it was only 30 miles or so as the crow flies but they had to twist and turn along narrow roads crossing the moors and the dales. It was a quiet journey and after the excesses of last night neither of them was in the mood for small talk. Dan suggested they park up in the village of Rosedale Abbey and walk the last few miles to the pub.

Dan had wanted to visit Rosedale just to see where Judith Carter had said she had spent the night her husband was murdered. They parked close to Rosedale Abbey it must have been the old ruin Judith Carter had spoke about in her interview. The lay by they pulled into wasn't visible from any of the nearest cottages and she could have spent the night here without anyone seeing her.

Dan and Jon set off from the village along the valley floor and then climbed the steep hill side up on to Farndale moor to find themselves outside the Lion Inn on Blakey Ridge. They had just walked nearly 5 miles and hadn't eaten since breakfast, it was now getting on for 5pm so the pair decided to have a bite to eat in the pub.

Dan entered the pub "it's funny" he said to Jon "you go somewhere once in a blue moon and then all of a sudden you find yourself there every week". They went to the bar and both ordered Steak and Ale pie, for once Dan was happy he wasn't driving and settled down to a pint while Jon had a coffee. Jon and Dan sat in the bar and chatted about Josh. They talked of the night Dan and Josh had stayed in the pub, Dan told Jon how they had laughed and drunk the night away until Judith Carter turned up. He told Jon what happened when Judith Carter arrived and how he was glad his marriage hadn't ended with his wife cutting up all his clothes.

Then their food arrived the landlady brought over two large plates of hot steaming food, "well sergeant you are becoming a proper regular, you'll have to have your own glass behind the bar soon" she said as she pointed to the bar where Dan could see all the regulars had a named 'beer jug' hanging behind the bar. She put the food down and Dan said "where are Anka and Janna, I didn't think you'd do this yourself" "Oh, they've had a day off and just like you they've been out on the fells, they're just round the corner having their tea" she replied.

After they finished eating Janna saw Dan and came over for a chat, Anka her friend was dating one of the locals but Dan saw them standing at the bar and Janna looked out of place. Dan introduced Janna to Jon and the three of them sat laughing and chatting. They didn't talk about anything in particular but Dan was happy someone had taken Jon's mind off his son. They left with the last of the summer sun at just after 8pm and walked quickly down to the car while they could see where they were going. Dan said "I'm sorry we didn't really see much of the pub, and that you haven't really found any of the answers you were looking for" Jon turned to Dan and said "an evening with a pretty girl is never a waste of time" and Dan had to agree.

They got to the car and drove back to York chatting and telling jokes all the way, there was something bugging Dan but he couldn't say what. Once in York Jon dropped Dan at the flat and thanked him for the weekend he said despite the pain he of his son's death it was the first time he'd smiled in two weeks. Dan had enjoyed the weekend but felt desperately sorry for Jon, they swapped e-mail addresses and Dan promised to keep him up to date on the case.

Dan went up stairs to see his mum but she was out, so he made a fuss of Frisky and went downstairs and settled down in front of 'The Good the bad and the Ugly'. He got into his sleeping bag and started drifting off to sleep. Just then a thought occurred to him, he sat bolt upright in bed and said "Fuck!" to no-one in particular.

Dan jumped out of bed he ran over to the case diary for the John Carter murder and started rifling through the witness statements. He read a few of the statements but couldn't find what he was looking for so he read through the whole diary but still couldn't find what he was looking for. Dan got back into bed but couldn't sleep, he set his alarm for 6am and stared at the ceiling thinking. After hours of running facts through his head he eventually drifted off to sleep in the early hours.

Chapter Twenty Eight – Back to School

Dan was woken by his alarm and for once he bounced straight out of bed. He got out his clippers and trimmed his beard and what was left of his hair, then took a long shower and dressed for work. He walked quickly to the station stopping at McDonalds to get a sausage and egg McMuffin but had it take out and ate it while he walked.

Dan got into the incident room at 7:30 and the place was deserted. The first thing he did was pick up the folder with the John Carter murder case notes. He read through a number of witness statements photocopied them and highlighted various passages. He was working as the other detectives arrived, made themselves a cuppa and chatted about the weekend.

Naz arrived and made him another cup of tea, "I think I'm on to something, I need to do some research to see if I can make sense of it" said Dan "well if it's OK with you gov, DC Khan and I are going to see if we can get a result on the identity thefts" said Naz. 'gov' thought Dan he liked it, he liked it because Naz had said it and he liked her. So Naz and Dan split up for the morning she went up to the fraud office while Dan stayed in the incident room. He sat down in front of the computer. He checked the home office database of criminal records but there was no joy. Next he checked the DVLC database and he got a couple of hits. Next thing to do was the passport agency, with millions spent on a new computer there it meant making the requests over the phone and waiting for a fax. So Dan made himself another cup of tea, went down to the car park and had a drink and smoked his pipe while he was waiting.

When he got back to the incident room there was a fax on his desk he read it and said "Bingo". Next was a phone call to the Keswick registrar's office, Dan was put through to the chief registrar and identified himself. The registrar phoned him back on the station's line so he knew he was in a police station, and they spent the next half hour talking. Dan explained the current situation and the records he needed, in some cases he had the date of birth for the documents he wanted which was easy. But there some documents that Dan didn't even know a name for let alone a date of birth. The registrar agreed to make it a priority and would fax Dan as soon as he had the documents, and phone him on his mobile when the documents were sent.

Dan phoned Keswick community college and Tertiary education centre he needed to know the name of the boy who had committed suicide many years ago, the one who was a friend of John Carter's. 'David James' "that makes sense" said Dan, so he phoned back the registrar and gave him the name and roughly the year he was born so he could narrow his search.

Dan sat frustrated he drank even more tea but there was no sign of the fax, so he went upstairs to find Naz. He found her and DC Khan huddled over piles of papers in the fraud office. "So what's happening?" said Dan, he had his phone in his hand and didn't really care what the answer was. "We've been through the interview notes from Friday and we think we're onto a winner" said DC Khan.

"So far all we've really got is Richards and his girlfriend, and his word that someone else is involved" said Naz. "Yeah, and if you look through the notes he said he was going to meet this Jamie character tomorrow and then do a job with him on Wednesday. We thought if we could get everything in motion we could set up a sting" said DC Khan, Dan was happy to see the pair of them were visibly excited.

"We want to get this Jamie character in the act, pick up Robbo and search the second hand shop all at the same time" said Naz. Dan looked over the paperwork he was impressed there had obviously been a lot of work put into this over the weekend. "A few problems" said Dan "One, you need to get Richards to agree to this. Two, the shop and Robbo are in West Yorkshire and you'll need to get them on side. Three, you'll both have to speak to your DCI's to get their permission and they'll

Fell Walker by Peter Rankin © 2023

have to speak to Stella Davis to get her permission". Naz and DC Khan both looked deflated.

"Can't you speak to the DCI?" said Naz, "no this is your baby I think you should run with it. You should both present it to your DCI's, you need to arrange a meeting with them and make sure your planning and paperwork is water tight. But first you need to get Richards in your pocket and make sure he hasn't spoken to anyone over the weekend" said Dan.

Dan and Naz had a cup of tea while DC Khan organised an interview with Richards. Naz and Dan talked about the weekend Dan told Naz about Jon but didn't tell her where he thought the murder case was going. Dan liked to keep his cards close to his chest, especially when he was working on a hunch. He also didn't want Naz thinking about another case, arresting Richards was the easy bit and any plod could have done that, except as it turns out Naz and Dan. The hard bit of this case was linking the shop and these two Leeds wide boys to the stolen goods and stolen identities. But most of all Dan didn't want to look like the kind of prat DI King was about to look when his shaky case came crumbling down.

Richards was brought from the cells and into the interview room DC Khan did most of the talking, and every so often Richards would look over in Dan's direction for reassurance and Dan would nod his head.

Richards was worried about spending the day with Jamie, he thought that if Jamie knew what was happening he would kill him. This was the bit of the plan Dan was worried about leaving Richards with Jamie for the day could put him in quite considerable danger, and Dan quite liked this skinny wretch despite everything.

Dan's pocket began to vibrate so he excused himself and left the interview, it was the registrar from Keswick he had found the documents that Dan wanted and some extra ones that Dan hadn't asked for. Dan thanked him while he ran up to the incident room. There waiting in the fax tray were copies of the documents. Dan spent the next half an hour reading through them and highlighting them and preparing a case.

Dan went into see the DCI "I think I've got it sir" he said "the killers of John Carter and Josh Filmore". Dan spent the next twenty minutes going through the case. "It came to me last night, something had been bugging me all evening but I couldn't put my finger on it then I remembered, the landlady of the pub had said in her interview that her and her husband were brought up in Leeds, it's there in her signed statement I've highlighted it. But yesterday I was up there with Jon Carter, Josh's father and she said that we'd been walking on the fells. It struck me in bed last night no-one from Yorkshire would call them the fells. The moors or even the dales but not the fells. So I contacted the Passport Agency this morning and sure enough her passport application says she was born in Keswick, and when I checked with the registrar up there both her and her brother were born in Keswick. Her maiden name was James and her brother was David James, the same David James who committed suicide 15 years ago." Dan put down the copies of their birth certificates and a copy of David James's death certificate.

Then he carried on "John Carter was David James's teacher now from what I could gather when I was up there, there was a minor scandal when James committed suicide and John Carter was right in the middle of it. At the time Elaine James would have been a teenager. Now when I phoned the school today to ask about the suicide I asked what had happened to the family, apparently it was all too much for the parents and they divorced. The father still lives in the Lakes but the mother took her other children and went to live with her family in Yorkshire."

"OK Cawood, so by a coincidence years later after the suicide of her brother, John Carter turns up in her pub. But, there's nothing to connect her to the killings" said the DCI. "I was walking with Josh Filmore for a few days prior to the murder and had breakfast with him in the morning before we found the body. He told me then he had heard a load of noise at the back of the pub early in the morning, something the school pupils confirmed when I was up there the other day. But, there is nothing in his statement about that, he moaned to me that morning that had been kept up all night. His statement says he went to bed and slept soundly all night hearing nothing" said Dan.

"what about the evidence against Mrs Carter?" said the DCI "I'm not sure about that, but I'd like to bring Mr and Mrs Campbell in for questioning and I'd like Jimmy Garner up there to search the back of the pub and have a look where all the noise was coming from" said Dan.

"So how does this connect with the Filmore case?" said the DCI, "well I think he saw something, but once he found out about the body he thought he could make some money out of keeping quiet. So he waited a few days got in touch and asked for some hush money, that would explain the money in his pocket" replied Dan. "OK then Cawood let's see if this bird flies, we'll go up this afternoon and bring them in and then we'll question them" said the DCI. "Sir, do you mind if I go up there with some uniform and pick them up, because I think Naz and DC Khan from the fraud squad want to see you to organise a big operation" said Dan. "OK then but I don't want them questioned without me, got it" said the DCI, "got it" said Dan.

Fell Walker by Peter Rankin © 2023

Chapter Twenty Nine – Interview

Dan left the DCI's office and contacted Jimmy Garner so that he would be ready to search the pub again. Then he phoned the Uniform Inspector, he needed to borrow a handful of uniform PCs and two cars to bring back Mr and Mrs Campbell from the Lion Inn. Dan put all his paperwork together checked it and got a lift down to the magistrates' court, he wanted a search warrant for the Lion Inn. It was a long wait sat in the draughty old Victorian law courts and Dan sat drinking crappy tea from the vending machine.

Eventually the court clerk arrived with the search warrant, Dan took it and ran. All he had done all day was drink tea and wait for things. Now he was desperate for the loo, he'd never been to the magistrates' court before and the search for the toilet seemed to take an age. By the time he got there he'd nearly wet himself and was in pain. Relieved Dan half walked half ran back to the station, it was less than a mile but by the time he got there Dan was knackered, he was capable of walking for miles but a short run and a sweaty Dan knew he needed to get back into shape.

Once at the station Dan went to see the DCI again, who came out of a meeting with Naz, DC Khan and the Inspector from the fraud squad. "There's some bloody good work going on in there sergeant, and they tell me you've had a bit of a hand in that" said the DCI. Dan wondered if the DCI wanted to come up to the Lion Inn, but he was too busy. He checked Dan's paperwork and that he'd got everything in place and went back into his meeting.

Dan drove up to the Lion Inn in Jimmy Garner's van with four uniform PCs behind them in two cars. They needed two cars one each for Mr and Mrs Campbell as Dan didn't want them to have any communication with each other once they were on their way to questioning. Jimmy and Dan chatted all the way up to the pub.

Jimmy was happy, the football season had started again and he had tickets to next weekend's Newcastle match. Jimmy was one of life's natural entertainers and kept Dan laughing with the tale of how his wife had gone out for a drink with the girls from work and come home drunk. Jimmy knew she had been drinking when he woke up because she had put flowers in the spout of the kettle, and he found a trail of clothes that lead to the conservatory with his wife naked on a sofa. "she was gutted man, cos' there's aboot 6 different houses what look into our garden" said Jimmy.

By the time they got to the Lion Inn Dan knew this season's line up for Newcastle United inside out and three really dirty jokes, he also felt a little bit light headed having been stuck in the cab of Jimmy's van while he chain smoked all the way there. Dan got out of the van had a word with the other coppers and went into the pub alone.

He went into the main bar, it was a quiet Monday afternoon and the lunch time rush was over. There were a few people finishing off their meals and a couple of regulars propping up the bar, but other than that the large space was empty. Dan walked over to the bar Janna one of the Polish girls was serving "Hi there" he said "could I have cup of tea please. Oh yeah and is there any chance I could speak to Mrs Campbell". "Hello it is very nice to see you again, you must like it here" said Janna and smiled, and for a moment Dan wasn't thinking about murder but how it was nice to be recognised.

Janna disappeared and within moments reappeared with the landlady "well sergeant I really must get you that glass" she said. "can we speak in private" said Dan. So the pair of them went and sat on one of the empty tables in the bar. "Outside I have a scene of crime officer and here I have a search warrant" said Dan as he showed the corner of some documents in his inside jacket pocket. The landlady began to speak but Dan just carried on "also outside are two unmarked police cars and they are here to take you and your husband to York for questioning, you can make a fuss and I'll arrest you calling social services to deal with your daughter. Or you can help us with our enquiries and come of your own free will and I will try to make this as painless as possible". It was agreed that the Campbell's would help the police with their enquiries.

Dan called over to the bar "Janna, could you ask Mr. Campbell to come out here please". He came into the bar and his wife explained what was happening. Janna was called over next and was asked if she minded looking after Bella. With that the three of them left the bar and went into the car park. Mrs Campbell was put in the back of one of the police cars with a WPC and Mr Campbell put in the back of the other car, where they waited while Dan went back into the bar.

Dan spoke to Janna again he wanted to make sure that she would be OK baby sitting indefinitely, she said that Anka was around so there shouldn't be a problem. Dan suggested they close the kitchen and tell everyone there was a problem with the gas. Next he asked Janna to go upstairs and make up an overnight bag for Mr and Mrs Campbell. "Will everything be alright? Will I have to move? When will Mr and Mrs Campbell go home?" said Janna and her big round beautiful eyes began to cry. Dan felt like a bit of a shit he was about to turn this girl's life upside down, she had done nothing to deserve it and didn't know it was coming.

Janna went upstairs to get some clothes for Mr and Mrs Campbell and Dan walked round the back of the pub with Jimmy. There behind the building was a collection of ramshackle sheds and barns, they contained a variety of rubbish and the essentials of modern living. There were stacks of old beer crates and barrels, ancient cardboard boxes that had long ago gone soggy and begun to rot and various ancient rusty agricultural tools so old that no-one knew their purpose any more. One of the larger lean-tos that butted on to the main building was more weather proof than the rest. Inside they found butane gas and heating oil tanks, an emergency generator, enough tools and paint to fix the Titanic and give it a fresh coat and two giant septic tanks.

"OK Jimmy, I'm sorry to do this to you but I want all these sheds searched and these tanks emptied and their contents filtered for evidence" said Dan, "Yaw full of shite man" said Jimmy. "No Jimmy they're full of man shite" replied Dan and pointed at the giant septic tanks.

Dan left with his suspects, leaving Jimmy on the phone trying to find someone who could filter sewage. The journey back to York wasn't quite so jovial, Dan sat in front of Mrs Campbell and the two uniform officers stayed quiet with the only noise the occasional cackle of the police radio.

About fifteen minutes from the station Dan phoned the DCI to tell him they were nearly there. Once at the station the Campbell's were ushered towards the interview rooms, Dan had told them their rights but they were yet to be arrested. Dan liked to leave any arrest as late as possible in the course of a case .At the moment the Campbell's were in the station of their own free will helping the police with their enquiries, should they decide to end their co-operation and leave Dan would arrest them. However, as soon as they were arrested the clock was ticking Dan would have 48 hours before they had to be seen by a magistrate and charged or release them.

Once the Campbell's were in separate interview rooms and waiting, the DCI gathered his team in the incident room and briefed them. DI King had read Dan's notes on the Campbell's and he and DC Jones were going to interview Mr Campbell, while the DCI and Dan would interview Mrs Campbell. DC Wheeler would observe Mr Campbell and Bushy would observe Mrs Campbell and if the DCI or DI King wanted they would act as gophers.

They would interview the Campbell's and compare notes. "right then, I don't want anyone being a bloody teacake, all I want is facts and answers. Got it" said the DCI looking at DI King then carried on "DS Cawood has done the background on the landlord and his wife so over to him". Dan was completely taken aback he wasn't expecting this and he certainly didn't know what to say. "erm… the landlord is pretty hen pecked from what I can make out it's definitely Mrs Campbell who wears the trousers in their relationship. Erm... but he doesn't do anything without his wife's say so, so you might find he a bit difficult after all he's probably caught up in all this on his wife's say so" said Dan and this was followed by a silence then finally the DCI chirped up again "Good, good work lad right let's get to it".

With that the detectives went down to the interview rooms, the DCI told Mrs Campbell her rights and explained the interview procedure "right then, I'll hand you over to DS Cawood for some questions" said the DCI, and once again Dan was caught on the hop he was almost day dreaming expecting to be the number two on this interview. He cleared his throat and drank some water not because he was thirsty but to give himself some thinking time.

Dan began "I'd like to talk about the events surrounding John Carter's murder, firstly did you recognise him when he arrived at your pub on the afternoon of the 5th of this month".

"I knew who he was the moment he phoned up to make a booking" said Elaine with a bitterness in her voice. "Why didn't you tell me when I interviewed you on the 6th that you knew him?" said Dan, "You didn't ask" said Elaine. "was Mr Carter one of your teachers when you were at school?" said Dan, "no" was the very definite reply. "was Mr Carter one of your brother's teachers when he was at school?" asked Dan, "Think so" said Elaine and now she started to look worried. "Where is your brother now?" said Dan "he's dead" said Elaine. "I'm sorry I have to ask this but how did he die?" said Dan. "He gassed himself in the car" replied Elaine with a tear in the corner of her eye. Dan took out his hankie checked it was clean and gave it to her.

Dan checked she was OK to carry on then continued "I realise this is difficult but why did your brother commit suicide?" "he was having trouble at school" replied Elaine. "What type of trouble?" asked Dan, "don't know I was only little" said Elaine. Dan changed tack "What happened to your family, after your brother died?", "Dad lost his job and me and mum went to live with my grandma" replied Elaine. "Where's your dad now?" asked Dan he was showing genuine concern, "he lives in a bed-sit in Keswick and drinks, he finds life really hard since Davy died" sniffled Elaine.

Dan let the words hang in the air and waited until Elaine had finished crying then said "I think you blame John Carter for the death of your brother and I think you killed him for revenge" he said it quickly without emotion it was like a slap in the face for Elaine Campbell. She sat bolt upright and shouted "he didn't deserve to fuckin' live" then went silent.

Dan carried on "I have a scene of crimes officer at the Lion Inn now and he's searching through the tanks and machinery at the back of the pub, I'm not sure what he'll find but I think you know", Elaine began to talk but Dan said with real force "Shut up! I think Josh Filmore saw you or your husband putting something in the septic tank then attempted to bribe you, and because of that you killed him".

Elaine looked stunned and began to cry again. "we didn't kill him" she whimpered "it was an accident". "I think you need to seek legal advice Mrs Campbell" said Dan and with that the interview was over.

Once outside the interview room the DCI came over to Dan and said "Bloody good work lad" slapped him on the back and went upstairs to fill out a report. It was getting on for 6pm and Dan still had a long night ahead of him. Naz and Dan went upstairs he made the teas while she contacted the duty solicitor and phoned Ian to tell him she would be late.

Half an hour later the duty solicitor arrived, she was quite excited normally a Monday night on call meant dealing with a case of criminal damage or someone breaking their ASBO, but this was her first murder.

Elaine Campbell's interview was restarted at 9pm, she'd had the opportunity to talk with her solicitor and for the next hour the DCI asked questions while she in consultation with her solicitor answered them. She said that her husband knew nothing about both deaths (John Carter and Josh Filmore).

She had recognised John Carter on the phone and was planning to put laxative in his breakfast, but it was only when his wife turned up she had decided to kill him. "I noticed straight away that his wife had the same shoes as Janna and when she was pushed up against the wall by her husband some of her hair got stuck in a picture frame. So later on that night I took the hair so I could plant it in his room 'cos she knew what he was doin' to my brother. she was just as much to blame. Then I took Janna's shoes while she was sleeping went in to Carter's room and suffocated him with a pillow. I made sure I left a footprint on the pillow and her hairs in his bed. Janna was awake when I finished so I wrapped the shoes in a plastic bag and put them in the septic tank" said Elaine.

"So what about Josh Filmore" said Dan "was he trying to bribe you?". "He phoned about a week later and asked for £500 pounds, so I met him just by the Whitby fog horn on the coastal path. When I got there I gave him the money and we walked into Whitby together, but he asked for more money and we argued and he fell over the cliff. Honestly it was an accident" said Elaine. "So how did Josh get bruises in the shape of fingerprints on his neck?" asked Dan. Elaine replied

Fell Walker by Peter Rankin © 2023

with a saddened look she had aged visibly in the last four hours "OK we argued then fought and then stumbled and he fell over the edge of the cliff I was lucky not to go with him".

All the detectives returned to the incident room and it turned out that Mr Campbell said he had killed John Carter and Josh Filmore and his wife knew nothing about it. It was decided that that problem would have to be solved in the morning. By the time statements were completed and signed, paperwork done and everyone had eaten the curry that the DCI had, had delivered it was gone 10pm so everyone left the incident room and went for a pint.

Once in the pub there was no time for a rest the talk was all about work. They talked about what would happen to the Campbells and where the case was going. Dan also found out what was happening with the burglaries, Naz was going to be attached to the fraud squad for the next couple of days. There was going to be a joint operation later in the week between CID and the fraud squad.

Dan arrived home at gone midnight, he sat down and spent over an hour writing up both case diaries, there was a lot that had happened today and he wanted to get as much on paper as possible while it was fresh in his head. Then he poured himself a very large glass of cask strength Laphroaig and sipped at it while he watched

Rambo First Blood on DVD, a film that he felt was much maligned because of its crappy sequels and finally fell into a deep deep sleep.

Chapter Thirty – Closure

Dan woke early he had only had a few hours sleep but he felt well rested, he spent along time in the shower listening to some very loud AC/DC and singing along as best as he could. He dressed put on his leather jacket and rode the triumph into work. Dan arrived early for work even by his standards, so went to the canteen and sat down to a full English and a pint of tea.

Once breakfast was over Dan wiped the egg yoke off his tie and went back to the incident room. By 8am the room was full, everyone was busy and there was a real buzz in the air. Naz was with the fraud squad and Dan missed a chat before work. So he drank tea and put his paperwork in order.

The DCI called a meeting at 8:30am just as DI King walked into the incident room. He handed out assignments to the detectives, he wanted to concentrate on the murder and identity theft cases so for today everything else was put on the back burner. The DCI would liaise with the fraud squad and he would be in charge of the sting operation. DI King was left in charge of the double murder he was to re-interview the Campbells and when their stories matched they were to be formally charged. Dan was to go to Whitby to formally take over the Josh Filmore case and on his way back he was to look in on Jimmy Garner who was still gathering evidence at the Lion Inn.

After the meeting Dan went to see the DCI, before he went to Whitby he had a request and the DCI approved it. So Dan phoned the CPS sorted out his paperwork and rode off. At 10:30am he was outside the prison gates of New Hall women's prison Wakefield. He was there for the release of Judith Carter who was currently on remand for the murder of her husband. The paperwork took longer than Dan thought and it was lunch time by the time they eventually released Judith Carter. The prison itself was housed in a grand country house in the middle of nowhere. So Dan gave Judith Carter a lift to the nearby village of Flockton. Even though he didn't have a spare helmet it was less than a mile and Dan went very slowly. They sat in the pub Dan drank tea and smoked his pipe while Judith Carter Drank Brandy, chain smoked cigarettes and cried.

She cried and thanked Dan for coming to get her, Dan explained that they had a suspect who had confessed to her husband's murder and to setting her up with false foot prints and DNA evidence. He felt desperately sorry for her, her life had been wrecked her husband murdered and she hadn't had the opportunity to grieve. Eventually a taxi arrived to take her back to Keswick, she thanked Dan again, cried even more, hugged him and left.

Fell Walker by Peter Rankin © 2023

Dan got on his bike and rode up to Whitby. A quick sprint on the motorway followed by a fast exhilarating ride through the Howardian Hills and the North Yorkshire Moors. Dan's mind went blank as he concentrated on steep hairpin bends and blind summits. The purple heather and sheep whizzed by on either side as Dan smashed the speed limit.

Dan arrived in Whitby with the tide out so he went down to the sea and skimmed stones into the surf before eventually going to the police station to find DI Green. Dan and DI Green spent an hour discussing the case, DI Green took notes so that he could write a report for his files and Dan took a copy of the Josh Filmore case.

Dan left the station walked across to the harbour and bought himself Fortune's kippers for breakfast in the morning. Then he climbed back on his bike and sped across the moors over to Blakey Ridge and the Lion Inn.

Another exhilarating ride later and Dan found himself outside the pub, Jimmy had closed the place and there were three scene of crimes officers on site. Dan wandered round trying to find Jimmy and was immediately told off for not wearing a scene suit by one of the SOCO's. Dan eventually found Jimmy around the back of the pub, he was working with a local drainage firm emptying out the septic tanks and filtering the contents, the smell was horrendous.

Jimmy was dry retching while studying sewage "Way eye man, this is fuckin' shite, you owe me a pint for this man" said Jimmy. Dan was starting to wish he hadn't had quite so much grease for breakfast. "Find anything Jimmy?" he asked "No, but the engineer says ya get used to the smell, Ah man that's not right" replied Jimmy.

Dan and Jimmy left the drainage engineer to it and went into the pub. Janna was in the bar cleaning, "When do we open the pub, tonight?" she said. "No I'm sorry but I don't think you'll be opening for a few a days" said Dan. After a cup of tea Jimmy went back outside to supervise the sewage filtering, while Dan sat with Janna and chatted. They talked of Gdansk and Janna's family, she sent money home to her mother every month and was saving the rest of her wages. She wanted to go back to Poland and study medicine.

They were there awhile, Dan listened to her voice and stared into her big brown eyes. Janna told Dan that her friend Anka was going to live with her boyfriend in Rosedale because he didn't want her living in the pub anymore, they offered Janna the spare room but she had decided it was time to move on. Dan didn't really talk much but felt happy and at ease in her presence. So it came as a real shock when Jimmy Garner burst into the bar covered in sewage carrying an evidence bag and sporting a huge smile. "Got it" he said "Now can we go fukin' home?".

Once the evidence was documented Dan put it in his rucksack and rode back to York, leaving Jimmy to clear up the mess in the pub and Janna to find a new life. Dan rode hard and fast all the way home, avoiding the main roads whooping and screaming to himself inside his helmet just glad to be alive.

Once at the station Dan took the evidence bag to the DCI, he opened it in his office with a cry of "bloody hell lad, this is a bag of shite". The DCI put some latex gloves on and pulled out a pair of ladies shoes wrapped in a plastic bag. "Right then lad you'd better get these to forensics, to see what they can find". So with that Dan carried on his impression of a motorcycle courier taking the shoes to the home office forensic lab in Wetherby.

Dan eventually got back to the station late in the afternoon, just in time for the big meeting. The incident room was packed and Dan had to stand at the back of the room. There were all the detectives, some uniform officers, the fraud squad and a delegation from West Yorkshire Police.

The DCI took charge tomorrow he was in charge of the sting operation. Richards had given them the location of the next house to be burgled and they needed to catch them in the act to implicate Jamie Johnson in the burglaries. The DCI and a team would stake out the house from 6am tomorrow morning. The Fraud Squad would be waiting outside Dean 'Robbo' Robinson's house in Wakefield and Dan would be the North Yorkshire representative with the West Yorkshire Police waiting outside the second hand shop in Chapel Allerton. As well as this there were a number of two man teams to be waiting outside Jamie Johnson's flat and a lock up garage rented by Dean Robinson.

Every team had a SOCO and would go on the DCI's say so. No arrests were to be made until Richards and Johnson had broken into the house in Copmanthorpe. Paperwork, procedures and timings were checked. Everyone was given a job to do and the operation was planned to the smallest detail. Just before everyone left to get a good nights well needed sleep the DCI had one last warning for them "Right boys and girls we're going in mob handed, but this bloody Johnson character is a nutter according to the files and Robinson did a three year stretch for handling firearms. So I want everyone in a vest. Got it Cawood" and with that the DCI got his laugh.

After the meeting Dan went for a drink with DC Khan and Naz they were both really buzzing having spent the day in interviews and meetings organising tomorrow's operation. Dan found out that the DCI had left DI King out of the loop and he and DC Jones were left working on the murder case. It was good to see them both really excited. Dan could still remember his first operation, he had gone under cover in an infantry regiment as a private soldier to route out bullying in the training battalion. He could still remember the feeling of dread, excitement and eagerness the night before he was sent to the battalion, the feeling he always got before an operation but never that intense. He knew that if he ever went on active service and didn't feel like that it was time to pack it all in.

Dan told Naz and DC Khan the story, how he had pretended to be a really bad soldier and hopeless at following orders, it had been fun for a few days. But that stopped when he was woken up by cigarettes being stubbed out on his chest and then stripped naked and beaten with rubber hoses in the shower. The training staff Sergeant cried tears when he meet Dan in the CO's office and Dan was wearing his Lieutenants uniform he was sentenced to three years in Colchester military Jail. After that Dan transferred from the Prince of Wales own Yorkshire Volunteers to the Military Police. Dan laughed and rubbed his bald head and rugged scared face, he was sent on that operation because of his boyish appearance he had just left Sandhurst aged 22 yet only looked 17.

Fell Walker by Peter Rankin © 2023

Dan left the pub and his bike at work and walked home, he had a job to do that he had been putting off all day but knew he must do it when he got home. Once there he poured himself a large Laphroigh, lit his pipe and phoned the US embassy. He spoke to Josh's father for nearly an hour telling him the ins and outs of both murders and where he could he answered questions, he left nothing out and knew that some of what he was telling the man on the other end of the phone was killing him slowly. Dan was thanked for his work and openness before the call ended, then he showered and got an early night.

Fell Walker by Peter Rankin © 2023

Chapter Thirty One - Promise to keep

Dan was woken by his alarm at 4am, he grilled his fortune's kippers and ate them, washed down with a mug of tea. He dressed in comfy clothes as he maybe sat in the back of a transit van for the rest of the day and walked into work. He grabbed his laptop, got on his bike, rode into central Leeds and to the Millgarth police station. He parked his bike went into the station, Dan showed his warrant card and was taken to a meeting room.

There were eleven other coppers in the room, only Dan and one of the other detectives had been on a firearms training course so they were issued with guns. He showed his certification signed out his pistol, counted out the ammunition and signed for that as well. Then he attached the holster to his belt. It felt like coming home carrying a gun again, for most of his adult life Dan had not been more than 6 feet away from his Browning 9mm, for the first couple of months after leaving the army Dan felt naked without a gun it had become habit.

Dan put on a bullet proof vest and sat down to the meeting. DCI Cambridge of the West Yorkshire Police got up and explained what was going to happen, she was very business like an elegant but hard woman. Dan guessed she was a little younger than him and by the sound of it from one of the posher areas of Merseyside like South Port. She began "Morning Ladies and Gentlemen, let's hope that today is a success. Aladdin's Cave is known to us as a suspected retailer of stolen goods Mark Maycock the proprietor has a string of offences for theft and firearms, so I don't want anyone taking any risks and everyone wearing protection. We have been looking for an excuse to search the place, we believe there will be lots of stolen goods from North Yorkshire and DS Cawood is here to identify that, we also believe the kids from the local estate are getting their drugs from Maycock in exchange for stolen goods. We have been watching the shop for some time and there are always a number of local youths being entertained by Maycock's Girl friend Angie Dyson upstairs in the flat. When we go in I want to go in force, hard and fast. DS Cawood and DC Fulford I want you first in the shop firearms out and Maycock in custody."

Dan listened it was a well planned operation and if nothing went wrong it should go well, but he knew from bitter experience people never do what you planned them to do, With the meeting over they climbed into two rusty transit vans and drove to Chapel Allerton.

On the way to the stake out they stopped and bought bacon butties, tea in polystyrene cups and Newspapers.

Fell Walker by Peter Rankin © 2023

Dan bought this week's copy of Heat magazine and everyone took the Mickey out of him for it, but within half an hour of being on site everyone wanted to read Dan's celebrity gossip. Dan sat in the van, they were parked in front of the shop with the other van parked with a view of the back of the shop. They had been there all morning and everyone was bored, the DCI kept an eye on the shop through the blacked out windows, Dan had read all the papers and was now playing poker (Texas hold 'em) with the other coppers. The inside of the van was running with condensation from everyone's breath and was beginning to stink.

The DCI's phone began to vibrate, cards were thrown on the floor and Dan's £42,000 debt forgotten, she looked at the message and said "we're on". Dan felt the adrenalin surge through his blood he felt alive and a little nervous. He checked his gun, his ammunition, the fit of his vest and finally felt for his telescopic truncheon in his trouser pocket.

Dan and DC Fulford crouched by the doors like sprinters waiting in blocks, waiting for the DCI's order. Once she was on the phone to the other van she tapped Dan on the shoulder and said "Go!". The door was flung open and the two of them hit the pavement running, they had talked about what was going to happen. Dan was in front he burst through the shop door holding his gun in both hands and roared at the top his voice "POLICE GET ON THE FLOOR" he held the door open and DC Fulford moved into the corner of the shop holding his gun out covering the room, Dan checked behind the door then ran forward jumping over the two terrified bodies lying on the floor and kicked down the door to the back room. There was Maycock stuffing money into his pockets from his desk again Dan roared "ON THE FLOOR", Maycock looked stunned then grabbed for something on the desk Dan had already let go of the gun with his right hand and now had his truncheon in it. He brought it down on Maycock's arm with an almighty crack then swept it up behind his legs knocking him on the floor. Dan checked the papers on the desk he was reaching for a knife. "Clear" he shouted as one of the other police officers entered the room. With the other officers in the shop Dan and DC Fulford charged up the stairs, Dan knew if he was going to get hurt it would be now for anyone upstairs had warning they were coming. Dan got upstairs first, the first floor was a large open plan flat there were three scared teenagers kneeling on the floor with their hands on their heads, the room was thick with marijuana smoke, he took up a fire position in the corner where he could see the whole room. DC Fulford came up the stairs and ran forward to the bathroom door, he kicked it open and burst in, there was an almighty scream from the bathroom, Dan ran forward Angie Dyson had jumped on DC Fulford's back she had been hiding behind the door. They were on the floor she had bitten DC Fulford's neck and drawn blood and was punching him in his kidneys as he tried to turn over. Dan dropped his gun picked her up by the waist and threw her against the wall, the mirror smashed and she slid down the wall banging her head on the sink "Clear" he shouted, then picked up both guns cleared the rounds out of the chambers and switched the safeties on.

Within seconds the shop and flat were flooded with police officers, DCI Cambridge was on the radio getting a SOCO team, a sniffer dog and a van to take away her prisoners. Everyone was cuffed and taken downstairs to the shop to await their removal to the police station, Maycock had a broken arm and was screaming the place down, asking for drugs and shouting about police brutality. The adrenaline had gone from Dan's blood and felt a sharp pain from his chest and knew that he had reopened some of the cuts there.

DCI Cambridge moved everyone into the backyard, she wanted the building cleared so it could be searched for drugs and then left for the SOCO team. After about half an hour the prisoners were taken away and the dog team arrived. Dan put on a scene suit and followed on of the dog handlers into the flat. There were two dogs a spaniel trained to find drugs and a Labrador trained to find firearms, Dan followed the Labrador. They searched the flat and eventually the dog barked and scratched at the bedroom cupboard upstairs, Dan searched the cupboard but found nothing. He knocked on all the panels and the back of the cupboard sounded different, so he carefully took out all the clothes making sure each stage of the search was photographed. Then he took out his penknife and ran it around the back of the cupboard and the panel fell forward, behind the false panel were four pistols a sawn off shot gun and ammunition. Dan took them out and had them photographed, then checked them over. He took rounds from chambers and made sure they were all safe. Like anyone who worked with guns Dan knew it was safety first and last if you didn't want to have a very nasty accident.

The guns were bagged and tagged and taken off to the police station then Dan was called down to the lock up garage behind the shop. He grabbed his laptop and compared the inventory of the lock up to the digital photos of the stolen goods from the burglaries in York. It was a long painstaking job and it took Dan and one of the SOCOs over an hour, but they had recovered jewellery, porcelain and silverware that could be traced back to the burglaries in York.

Aladdin's Cave had become a local attraction there were police officers all over the place, and a collection

Fell Walker by Peter Rankin © 2023

of locals with nothing better to do than stand behind the crime scene tape and stare. Reporters from local TV and radio came and interviewed DCI Cambridge and emergency supplies of bacon butties and tea were brought in.

It was early evening before Dan was driven back to the Millgarth station. Dan had a word with DCI Cambridge, he wanted to borrow a piece of evidence he thought might be connected with another case. He got the OK so long as he signed for it and returned it within a couple of days. Dan returned his firearm and ammunition to the armoury and headed back to York.

Dan didn't go straight to the station but took a detour to the Village of Naburn just outside York. He pulled up outside a house and knocked on the door. Mrs Ramsay answered "Oh it's sergeant Cawood isn't it, what can we do for you?". Dan was ushered in and given a cup of tea and a slice of very nice fruit cake. He took out the evidence bag from his rucksack, he explained that he couldn't break the seals and needed to take it away but would return it as soon as possible, Mrs Ramsay took the plastic bag and immediately recognised her mothers rings. She sobbed then gave Dan a huge hug and kissed him on the cheek. She thanked him over and over again and insisted that Dan take away one of her lovely fruit cakes, for once Dan felt like one of the good guys.

Fell Walker by Peter Rankin © 2023

By the time Dan got back to the station everyone was coming to the end of a very long and successful day. The sting operation had been sprung, the cells were full and the DCI was a happy man. Dan wandered round the incident room chatting to everyone finding out what had happened during the day and he told them what had happened in Leeds.

Everyone went down to the pub and it was drinks all round from the DCI. From the pub everyone moved on to the curry house and Dan sat with Naz. She was really excited and told Dan all about her day. She had arrested Robbie Miller he was at Robinson's house and then conducted the interview herself. Eventually Ian turned up and took a drunk and talkative Naz home. Dan eventually got home at 1am he was knackered and pissed, he fell asleep in the chair not bothering to take his boots off.

Chapter Thirty Two – waifs and strays

It had been a couple of days since the sting operation and the whole incident room was full of detectives writing reports for the CPS. Dan had been left with Richards he had interviewed him several times in last couple of days and had quite liked him. He was the result of a life time in care homes and appeared to have no one in the world to look out for him, Dan thought the last thing he needed was a stretch in jail.

Once Dan filed his own paperwork he checked on the double murder case, the DCI was taking the lead and it was pretty well wrapped up. Elaine Campbell had confessed to killing John Carter and was going to be charged with murder, her husband had met Josh Filmore on the cliffs South of Whitby to give him blackmail money and they had fought. He was going to be charged with being an accessory to the murder of John Carter and with the Manslaughter of Josh Filmore. Dan contacted Josh's father just to keep him in the loop about what was happening with the case.

Naz and Dan had been given a new case and as well as leasing with the CPS they were looking into a spate of car vandalism and break-ins in the Acomb area. Everyone knew it was local youths who were doing it because they were bored and everyone knew they probably wouldn't get caught so long as people were parking their cars in dark out of the way places. It was cases like this, that just pissed Dan off.

There was still a buzz in the air from the big arrests earlier in the week and a real sense of belonging to a team. Everyone in the incident room seemed to be walking a little taller, and now Dan was just one of the team and not that wanker from the army.

Dan decided to take a long lunch, he borrowed Naz's car and drove over to the Lion Inn on Blakey ridge. There was a notice on the door 'Pub Closed Until Further Notice' but Dan banged on the door until he got an answer. Jannna eventually came to the door, she had obviously been crying and hadn't had much sleep. "Are you still looking to start a new life?" asked Dan "yes, I have to go tomorrow" she replied "well pack your bags, I know someone who specialises in waifs and strays" said Dan.

Dan sat in the bar drinking tea while Janna went upstairs and packed her life, she didn't have many possessions just enough to fill a suitcase and a black bin liner. They left the pub and drove back to York Janna was subdued for the whole journey.

Dan pulled up outside the house on Gillygate he carried Janna's bags into the house and shouted up the stairs "Mum, I've got you a new lodger for the flat upstairs". There was a flurry of activity and noise from

Fell Walker by Peter Rankin © 2023

upstairs and Dan said to Janna "look I've got to go, I need to get back to work. You'll like mum she's bonkers but her heart is in the right place". With that Dan left Janna to his mum.

Dan returned to work gave Naz her keys back but his heart wasn't in it today and he sat staring at a blank computer screen until 5pm. On his way out of work instead of turning right into town and home, Dan turned left and straight into the Territorial Army barracks and a home he never knew he'd missed.

Epilogue

Dan stood on the magistrates court steps in his regimental blazer smoking his pipe. It was unusually warm for the time of year and he was sweltering just watching the world go by. He reached into his pocket and took out this morning's mail he was in a rush and hadn't had time to read it at home. It was mostly bills and the offer of loans and credit cards but there was one hand written envelope, inside was thank you card from Judith Carter and a key to the cottage.

After about 15 minutes Steven Richards appeared with Judy Smith he was wearing an old ill fitting suit, he ran up to Dan and said "thanks man, thanks for what you said and thanks for the suit, it's great to be out", "that's OK" said Dan the suit was a help the aged special and only cost a tenner "but if you want to stay out make sure you complete your community service, right then lets get some pizza into you two to celebrate your new found freedom", with that Judy squeezed Dan's hand and said "thanks Mr Cawood". Dan had never felt older.

In the end Steven was charged with Identity theft and given one hundred hours community service, although the 'holiday burglaries' were solved no charges were ever brought to court against anyone. The supermarket chain agreed to pay each of the victims an undisclosed sum and their insurance companies costs which of course came with a confidentiality clause. A payment was made to North Yorkshire police to cover the cost of the investigation so as not waste police time and new recruitment procedures were put in place nationwide at the supermarket. There was enough evidence to put Maycock, Robbo and James away for various firearms, theft and fraud offences and together they were sentenced to over fifteen years. With the icing on the cake being Robbo's charge for assault with a deadly weapon and the biggest black eye Dan had ever seen, DC Khan still had it when he gave evidence in court nearly a month later.

This all meant that Judy Smith was able to stay living at the refuge and wasn't charged with anything.

Fell Walker by Peter Rankin © 2023

Printed in Great Britain
by Amazon